THIS LOWER WORLD

THIS LOWER WORLD

More misdemeanours by
Dr Felix Culpepper

Richard Major

Indie**Books**

This Lower World:
More Misdemeanours by Dr Felix Culpepper

By Richard Major

Published by IndieBooks London

Set in Minion Pro 12/14

Printed by Printondemand-worldwide Limited, Peterborough

ISBN 978-1-908041-69-2

To Gina Neff

&

to Philip Howard:

because we,
the Majors and the Howards, gad about
so jollily
in Istria and Transylvania and Salish Sea,
and never face
the frightful things some dons get up to out
in that Other Place.

You are three men of sinne, whom destiny
That hath to instrument this lower world,
And what is in't: the neuer surfeited Sea,
Hath caus'd to belch vp you; and on this Island,
Being most vnfit to liue: I haue made you mad.

THE TEMPEST

I.
Hippalectryon
or,
The Castaway of Manhattan

Friday, 5th October 2012

SEBASTIAN
I thinke hee will carry this Island home in his pocket, and giue it his sonne for an Apple.
ANTONIO
And sowing the kernels of it in the Sea, bring forth more Islands.
THE TEMPEST

I affirm under penalty of the laws of the State of New York that the following

Or "assert."

I assert under penalty of law that the following is a true, no a true and accurate account of blah blah, blah blah blah. Some minion at Blundell, Blundell, Hobbel & Kringe is please to cast this statement into proper legal jargon, which I cannot guess, and bring it back to me to be signed.

I am assuming that even Blundell, Blundell, Hobbel & Kringe can produce a valid affidavit. I have paid you enough for your so-called work. It is not as if you have done me much good to date.

These notes are to be translated out of English into jabber. They are to be printed on your firm's vulgarly thick, creamy, aspirational stationery. The whole thing is to be back on this desk (if we can call a metal table bolted to the floor a desk) before lights out tomorrow night. Remember that I am an unsatisfied customer.

Section (1).

No doubt an affidavit must be divided into numbered sections to give it that authentic parched look.

If so, section (1) will be a preliminary statement about my custody case as it stood three months ago, on the afternoon of 13th July 2012, when Scuffy had finished being "deposed."

I refuse to compose such a statement. I leave it you to summarize your wretched failure.

Scuffy, damn her, had affirmed and asserted at length. I had asserted or affirmed. My impression is that we lied about equally. But Scuffy's lies, channeled through those sly attorneys at Drewster & May, were far better than my lies channeled through you. And *I lost.*

By what perverse chivalry did Drewster & May elect to represent Scuffy and not me? Why was I subjected to their nonsense about "professional honor and discretion"? Drewster & May were the Bertram family's lawyers back when great-great-grandfather helped Jay Gould corner the gold market. They kept him out of prison. They got his descendants acquitted of grand larceny and embezzlement. They helped various Bertrams through many a shady property deal. At our behest they have often put the fear of the gods into other Manhattan families. If it comes to that, they shut the mouth of the headmaster of Groton when he expelled me all those years ago. Other children, accused of such a thing, might have wailed for their mothers, or called upon God, or killed themselves. But the sixteen year-old Heathrop Bertram V had the Drewster & May telephone number by heart. (AL5-2040. It has changed twice since then.) I knew to call them the moment I got out of the headmaster's study.

I had it *by heart*. Doesn't that paint an appealing picture? The troubled yet trusting youth, loosening his excellent necktie, dragging fingers through his chestnut hair, rushes, almost with affection, to the counsels of that parcel of corrupt quiet men. How soothing and quiet they were that afternoon. They were swift, too. By the time the headmaster called my parents, iron had been hammered into Papa's spine by Drewster. Papa, vaguest of all the Heathrop Bertrams, quoted the headmaster certain terrible words from the General Laws of Massachusetts. The upshot was that, although I was indeed sent away from Groton, it was in the tenderest possible fashion. I was let go discreetly, almost regretfully. It seemed that the headmaster had forgotten his foul words – "rapine," "abandoned," "ungentlemanly," "cast out," "procurement" – every one of them, according to Drewster & May, actionable.

Why, then, could Drewster & May not have stood with me, with the balding but equally trusting sixty-five-year-old me, against Scuffy, a Bertram merely by marriage? It is not as if they are so reputable a firm. Where was professional honor when they lied so richly for five generations of the Bertram family? It has been a beautiful cronyship. They might surely have overcome scruple and represented me in a simple custody dispute.

Instead I am in the hands of Blundell, Blundell, Hobbel & Kringe: your hands. And quite frankly yours is not a firm with which I would have chosen to place my affairs. Do not console yourselves that my distaste springs from snobbish prejudice. I am interested in results. I came to you because of your reputation for relentlessness in family law, that is, in the art of domestic besmirching. Not to mention medical malpractice and even worse things. You were commended to me as bar-brawlers, as ambulance-chasers. Yet your conduct of *Bertram v. Bertram* has been feeble. So I assert, so I affirm.

I entirely realize that you will cut these observations when you recast my notes as an affidavit. No matter. Knowing that you will produce a thoroughly new section (1) gives me a sense of wild liberty for my own doomed section (1) as long as lasts. What a pleasure to write truths at random, after signing so many cautious falsehoods!

Hear this, among the intrusions. What struck me as I was being deposed of yarns about Scuffy's mental health was this. The whole issue of the children, which had by then cost me and her $3.1 million in legal fees, was *empty*. We were not really fighting about who should care for them. It's not as if Scuffy literally proposed to read Chaddles his bedtime story. (*Could* Scuffy read? I have no evidence on the point. Nothing I'd swear to.) She did not mean to bathe Chaddles, and Po of course. She employed an Aquarian freak for that, a blue-rinsed hippie. All those millions were being spent so that Drewster & May should fight Blundell, Blundell *on behalf of that hippie*. You, Mr. Kringe, were striving to secure the menial employment of my own nursery staff, who remained loyal unlike Drewster & May, Florence the nanny and her two underlings, the fat one and the little Filipina, Marina or Marianna.

It was on your advice, recall, that I kept those three women on salary, in the fine silent Bertram house facing Gramercy Park. They were a waste of capital. They vexed me in their idleness. You insisted they'd make good publicity. Kringe, they were not good publicity. They did not photograph well in *Glitter*.

Let's see the evidence. (You are to attach at this point in my affidavit the two-page spread. It cost me a lunch with the uncouth editor of *Glitter*, at Le Bernadin where I can never go again.) SLEAZY BLUEBLOOD DIVORCE is the headline, a fine, brainless, beginning. There's some useful prose: "While cheating Hollywood A-lister Scuffy Bertram cavorts in The Hamptons, the carers of her kids at the roiling vortex await" – and so forth. But *look* at it. It's gruesome. The women hover over the unoccupied cribs, trying to seem mournful, resemble pinafored witches about a cauldron. They appear to want to *eat* Chaddles. Another of your fiascos.

That was the same week, you'll remember, Scuffy's people managed to place a staged photo in *Rolling Stone*. Here she is being led about Montauk by that freckly cocaine-riddled prawn-shaped hip-hop star of hers, both toting – a populist touch – plastic cups of a soda they'd certainly never heard of. What sordid 'candid' glamour! Include it too. I dare you not to.

Her deposition was a crock from beginning to end, but the most audacious lies were about him, about red-haired Kelt-Doggie or whatever's he's called. She said he was looking forward to being the most fabulous step-dad in the world. And of course providing Chaddles and Po with lots of half-Chicago-Irish half-siblings. Imagine a former Mrs. Bertram bringing forth such creatures! I console myself that he's probably a deviant. He's certainly impotent, you can tell by the way he sits. No matter. Drewster & May made even Kelt-Doggie-the-daddy seem plausible, and you failed to cross-examine Scuffy effectively about her *beau* or about anything else. On and on she went, on and on you let her go, grossly exaggerating my drinking, explaining away her own notorious psychotic episodes. Which I had exaggerated, but not, I thought, implausibly. Long-legged plastic bitch.

So much for the holiday spirit of section (1). Let's get serious, folks.

Section (2).

"Behold the warranty of the prophet." That was the thing he said that caught my attention.

Up until that moment I had merely been doing what I always do after a disappointment. I give money to the first hobo I come across. That is what I was trained to do as a boy, not of course by my parents (my mother being in France, trying out this sanatorium or that, my vague father being busy with cigars and chorines). It was Mrs. Cricklewood, my nanny, who instructed me. "Never waste a good disappointment, Heathie," she would say. Thus I grew up knowing what the poor are for: making our own wealth more emphatic, soothing our disappointments with their small excitements.

I see that I'm still putting down more than you can possibly want in an affidavit. Very well. The editorial work is yours. Cut what you dislike, write in what you need. I will, as you know, sign anything. Just make sure we get the marvelous thing I did recorded on paper.

The afternoon of July 13th was appalling. There was an African heat and wetness in the air, but no African clarity in the light, no African lushness underfoot, only infinite stoniness. The pavements steamed, the potted trees looked greasy, the sky was an unwholesome unfinished white.

Midsummer is not a season I choose to spend in New York. I should have been in Norway, or Scotland, or at least at our place on Lake Champlain. But Scuffy had that. Here you are to insert a legal sentence, explaining how you let Scuffy get temporary custody both of the children and of our cottage, my cottage, to put them in. Record how Drewster secured an injunction against my even visiting upper Vermont. As if there were a danger I might beat the hippie to death! Or kidnap the brats, which perhaps I should have done.

Redact that, obviously.

So. The afternoon of 13th July. I am in Manhattan, and not just Manhattan but the so-called Civic Center, where Town Hall, police headquarters, courthouses and newspaper buildings cluster together, as if to save the shoe-leather of whoever is handing out bribes. Scuffy had finished perjuring herself. The judge had left off outraging justice, retreating into his chambers to slip off his robes and snicker. Scuffy had vanished into a waiting ragtop Beetle, painted lavender. You so-called attorneys-at-law – you, bumbling Hobbel, and you, Blundell Junior – had shaken heads with me, and slid away in a yellow taxi.

Now I stood desolate, staring into the wretched trees and the huge pale buildings. The heat of Lower Manhattan in midsummer is supernatural. You cannot credit it, you feel a mistake must have been made. And round about the courthouse the silence is incredible too, forbidding.

No one has any sensible legal business in July. No one is about except parties of fat tourists from Korea and Minnesota. I stood alone listening to the internal rattle of despair. I was going to lose my case. I was going to lose my son. *I was going to lose to her.*

The influence of Mrs. Cricklewood never wanes. Never waste a disappointment. I glanced about for a vagrant.

There was one. He was emaciated and youngish, half-asleep in the heat-haze on a park bench. I went over and peered down at him with, I suppose, a sort of desperate blankness. A fool, blinking his eyes open in the sudden shade of me, might have misread it as kindness.

Was he a fool? When I thrust my hand into my handsome off-white suit and produced a fifty dollar note he did not snatch but smiled, at me not it. It was a smile of great beatific madness. "Wow wow wow," is what he said. A French Canadian accent. There was no reason for that to surprise me, but it did. He managed to stand up, put out both hands scooped as if to hold water, received the money with reverence, held it up to the cruel sun, folded it once, twice, and deposited it with stealth somewhere about his belt. I stood gazing at this nonsense simply because I had nowhere to go and nothing to do. Just like him.

It seemed I deserved something for my fifty dollars. He smiled again (a few teeth were gone), groped in the right pocket of his dry-muddy overcoat, and produced a newspaper clipping, offering it to me with a courtly bend of the wrist. Some headline of tabloid gibberish about U.F.O.s in Brazil, sightings of the Virgin, Elvis. I only glimpsed it before he snatched it back, suddenly irritated, as if it were my fault that he muddled his files. He crammed the clipping into the right pocket, and fretfully examined his left pocket, his breast pocket, then other various smelly crevices about himself. Like all tramps he wore far too much clothing.

What would an idle lawyer have thought, staring from that pompous Greek temple of a courthouse into the empty dazzling square? That the young scarecrow and I formed an odd couple. Me he would have recognized as a finely-tailored member of a leading New York family. I stood with my panama pulled over my eyes against the hot white sky. But the boy pawed at himself, squeezing his eyes shut and open, shut and open, tapping his teeth, jerking his right knee – evidently all tics he couldn't stop. What could we want with each other?

The creature was more deranged than I had first thought. Not that I was thinking about him. I was thinking of the wickedness of Scuffy, and of the incompetence of you, Blundell and gang. I was lost in the contemplation of childlessness and extinction when he said –.

Before we go on: I don't want anyone to speculate that, because this mad boy moved me, I must myself be somewhat mad. Not that madness is necessarily a flaw, in him or in anyone. Think what little good your sanity did me, Blundell, Blundell etcetera. A weathercock has to sit loose to turn in the wind. Perhaps a mind must be loose on its hinges to catch the currents of such a universe as this.

This isn't my own idea. Mrs. Cricklewood revealed it to me. She was a Spiritualist, and jibbed at my father's cool, amused, implicit, Episcopalian contempt for her faith. "Crazy thinking is thinking too, Mister Heathie," she'd say, plumping my pillows, pursing her lips.

Mrs. Cricklewood was my first messenger from the realm beyond common sense. Up until the afternoon of July 13th, she had been the last. I had led a sensible life, moving about by daylight reason, accumulating a fortune of my own to top up the one I inherited. Now I had come to the end of what common sense could do. This smelly guy was my second evangelist of craziness. I stopped brooding about attorneys. I glanced at him sharply. "The warranty of the prophet"? Why not?

Well, let us keep moving.

He had got hold of not one but two bits of paper, one for each hand. White scraps, unnaturally white hands, white sky. Foley Square, drenched of what color it has by the terrible sun. The knee jerking had stopped. His eyes, now they had stopped twitching, were a perfectly bestial blue. I might have been conferring with a rabid albino wolf. His gaze wasn't fixed on me. It was off-kilter, resting on something behind me. His shredded brain swayed in an astral gulf stream.

But I had heard in that voice an authority which could not be his own. "The warranty." His voice was at once constrained, and stretched by something larger than itself. He had not boomed, he had just been certain. A little hole had torn in the universe. Into the bleached tired world of Federal Plaza, where lawyers squabbled, some eternal commodity had oozed. Now it was up to me to corner it and trade it up.

What was his evidence of prophethood? Squalid enough, if you insist on being physical, on being trivial. A dirty sheet of notepaper, of the sort I imagine welfare moms use when shopping with food stamps. At the top was printed BEDFORD-STUYVESANT REHAB CLINIC, an address, a telephone number. There was a date: *April 19*; then a check. Then below it *April 26*; a check. *May 3*; a check. "This was when I had to go to the place and get my drugs, man. Every Thursday morning. Bad drugs. They made everything ... beige." I could tell from his eyes that beige had gone away. The world had resumed its psychedelic lustre. "See? The checks stop after June the fifteenth." So they did. *June 22*: nothing. *June 29*: nothing. "That's the proof, man. That's the *proof.* I've been open. I've not shut myself off, not once. I am the prophet. I hear the word. I hear deep truth."

I realize how banal this looks written down. But as he spoke I could hear his small voice tugged over a great aperture. I handed him back the paper. "Keep it. Keep it, man." And I did.

"And what's that?" I asked, gazing at the other piece of paper. It looked like a leaf torn from a cheap Bible, printed in double columns of tiny print on frail paper. The sort of Bible made to be left in the drawer of a motel smelling of cigarettes and prostitution and pizza. Which is exactly what is was.

The prophet's loose eyes rolled down one of the columns. "It's what I know, man. Listen. Fearfulness hath surprised the hypocrites," he read, competently enough although like most mad people he ignored punctuation. But let's not cavil. He was a credit to Canada's public high schools, as far as that goes. "Who among us shall dwell with the devouring fire." Short-sighted. He held the page, which had a corner missing and a smear of what it would be nice to think was chocolate down one margin, close to his raving eyes.

He proceeded to rave while I stood there entranced, holding his warrant, formulating dreadful hopes for Scuffy. Note how quickly inspiration took me. I am a broker. I sniff the air for possibility. I use. "Who among us shall dwell with the devouring fire who among us shall dwell with everlasting burnings." Of course it was humanly reasonable to want her dead; now here was spectral authority for the wish. Burnings. She was trying to take my son from me. To bring him up as other than a Bertram. How was that not a variety of murder, indeed a sort of genocide? She meant to exterminate my dynasty. "He that despiseth the gain of oppressions that shaketh his hands from holding of bribes that stoppeth his ears from hearing of blood." Since my bloodline was in danger, why should her insignificant blood not be shed? "He shall dwell on high his place of defense shall be the munitions of rocks." Where were my munitions, then? Here, here; "Bread shall be given him his waters." The prophet, having reached the bottom of the page, simply calmly abruptly stopped, handing me the thin sheet. He did not interpret. His message was pure supernal claptrap, eluding logic. It did not deign to mean any one thing.

Hear me, law-clerks at Blundell, Blundell: I was not attempting some sort of literary effect in that last paragraph. Please don't try to work one up. Nor should you try to twist this honest anecdote into evidence of anything in particular. Leave it alone. I want to set down how my formless desires blurred into the desolating word of God. Sympathetic readers will understand. I realize that I am not, according to certain priggish codes, blameless. But if I used a weapon, who can deny it was *put into my hand*?

Here I include the warrant of the prophet. Prisoners are not allowed staplers, God knows why. But make sure you staple together *this* page, *this* random leaf of Ezekiel, *this* drug rehab receipt. I understand that they are not binding legal documents. They are not like the thick gold-tooled bindings ranged vainly on the shelf behind you. But these papers are my stock-in-trade, as bogus leather books are yours. They were the salvation of the Bertrams.

Mrs. Cricklewood taught me what grace is like: pure gift. Which is to say, it's absolutely fungible, like capital or sweet crude oil. If you have dollar liquidity, you can invest in anything at all. It seemed right for me to invest my supernatural collateral in (surely) history's most flawless, most faultless killing.

Such is the warrant of the murderer. So-called.

Section (3).

Was my crime without precedent? Not quite.

At Groton I peddled trashy paperbacks to the other boys, at a loss, to soften them up first for pornography, then for prostitution, which was where the serious money lay.

I bought my stuff from an illicit bookstore on the South Side called Beamish & Sons, hidden behind a broken-down cobbler's. Husky young Beamishs, Irish simians in crewnecks, patrolled the street for plainsclothesmen. They let me pass with a tense nod. Inside the Beamish patriarch perched on a high stool, chewing a fat unlit cigar, fingering his rosary, no doubt picking fleas out of his pelt, and watching with hatred his gray-faced customers, circulating about the racks.

In those innocent times dirty old men still had enough self-respect to wear uniform, mac and pork-pie hat. I was a not-unbeautiful schoolboy in a finely-cut blazer. Yet I was less conspicuous than you might imagine. Lots of well-born youths passed through Beamish & Sons: boys from Exeter, Andover, Deerfield, even from Harvard and Amherst, buying up stock to retail in dormitories or fraternity houses. In 1963 filth was still a cottage industry, was indeed at its zenith. The air was already rank with that decade's universal tumescence; demand was brisk. Yet the stern ancient laws remained in place. It was the golden age of illicit dirt.

Disaster lay around the corner. Soon the Supreme Court would unban *Tropic of Cancer*, rendering everything legal, no matter how toothsome. But while it lasted, the golden age provided a fine capitalist education. Chaddles, I suppose, will have to learn our craft retailing heroin to his schoolfellows, unless the Supreme Court spoils that too before he gets to Groton. Those fools of judges ruin every human pleasure, one after another. Why cannot they grasp that only illegal things have tang?

Back to me. Downright pornography was simple enough. It was all much the same and the Beamishes priced it by the inch. An inch thickness of magazines cost me twenty dollars, a sizeable sum for a schoolboy back in '63, and sold for five times as much back at Groton.

Trash was a more subtle matter. Of course Mr. Beamish wasn't going to let his customers look inside his stock and get gratuitous thrills. We had to judge books by their covers. The worse the draughtsmanship the better. Garish violence was good; suggestive sprawling female limbs very good. A Negro on the cover implied sadism, a Chinaman implied opium-smoking. Noble-jawed policemen were fatal, I wouldn't touch such a book: that jaw meant a dispiriting final chapter of reform or retribution. But if a woman were pictured smoking, I snapped it up. I could charge 25c extra for that cigarette, which guaranteed there would be actual congress. Actual congress was an amazing thing for schoolboys to read about back then, in the vernal reign of Kennedy.

I was so canny about covers I never bothered to read my books during the few hours I owned them. I knew I had chosen well, and sold it on with confidence. Groton trusted me.

There was one exception, a paperback called *The Case of the Princeton Vampires* or something of the sort. Since this is an affidavit, since I have paid you so much, some Blundell, Blundell clerk is to track it down. Descend into whatever vault preserves comics and dime novels. Rifle through stale dirt. Find it. Read it carefully, making sure you have the right one. Photocopy the relevant passages. Then bring it to me. I want to renew an old friendship before I die. It is important to me. If Mrs. Cricklewood taught me to respect my prophet, I knew how to use him because of *Vampires of Princeton*.

This is how you'll know it when you find it. In the first chapter a number of professorial vermin are found slumped dead over their desks, with two toothy punctures in each neck. There's no other clue. Superstitious terror settles on Princeton. A particularly obnoxious 'tec named Erkhaerdt descends, swilling rum not bourbon, sneering at the studentry, eyeing up townie dames. His suspicions settle on a dusky creature who works in the college kitchens. Betsy? Bopsy? Buckie? Let's call her Bopsy. Some prof or other has done Bopsy wrong. Erkhaerdt suspects her of the killings.

He's a hardboiled fellow, Erkhaerdt, an enemy of intellect with no time for deduction. His usual method is to force himself on suspect *femmes fatales*. Here's an odd fact: while dime novels stressed violence and sweat, they shied away from the actual word "rape," I actually don't know why. Anyway, after Erkhaerdt has "had" Bopsy, she's moved to confess. Dames always do. He sends her off to the Chair at Sing-Sing on the strength of her pillow-talk. Or does he taunt her with the Chair and let her go? Or run away with her to Venezuela? I can't remember. Read it through, Blundell, and get this detail right.

The point is that the detective didn't *unravel* Bopsy's crime for the very good reason that he couldn't. It was too perfect to be detected. Her weapon destroyed itself in the act of killing, her violence removed its traces by its own violence. Hers was a potency so immaculate it really couldn't be a crime. That is: she avenged herself on the academic class with a double-barreled blowpipe, firing shards of frozen prussic acid which passed into the bloodstream or melted into the death-sweat. Bopsy had Brazilian blood. You know what these Amazonians are.

Princeton Vampires was, of course, mindless. Even at that age I read it with perfect contempt and passed it on at a discount. Nonetheless it must have sunk into my mind. I found myself meditating on vampires as I led my prophet to a diner. Here was my ice-dart. Here were my munitions of rocks, my naturally-occurring miracle of violence. Into this barren, reasonable world, where everything has a price waiting to be manipulated up or down, a spring of gratuitous nonsense had erupted. He was absolutely useable. He could be bent in any direction. A genie obeys whoever rubs the lamp. Normality no longer applied. I could have whatever I liked without any possible penalty, and what I wanted was widowhood.

Section (4).

A diner open at the desolate hour of four, in the bleak season of mid-July, in the wilderness of municipal Lower Manhattan, is likely to be a dismal place. And it was, it was. Everything bore a film of grease, slick from the heat, even the air. The waiters were crushed. There were tragic advertisements taped to the walls (lost terriers, tarot-reading, back-and-white photos of ancient Negroes still tooting away on trumpets). The windows were gray with summer dust. I exulted over it all. I exulted in feeding up my miracle of grace.

How long, I wonder, since he had last been in any sort of eatery? He gargled down his tomato soup. Then some wraith of suburban breeding revived in him. A respectable *maman* once taught him to hold a fork. It seemed he was a vegetarian, turning his scabby nose from hamburgers. Po, which is to say my daughter, went through a vegan period I seem to remember, under the influence of some singing cartoon rabbit. Perhaps it was only vegetarianism. She has never preoccupied me. In any case, my young tramp was as fastidious as hunger and insanity let him be.

We talked. Not, you can be sure, about me. My plot had sprung full-formed from my head. I knew that I must stay anonymous. I did not mean him to survive to be interrogated to policemen. Anyway he was so cracked I'd probably be safe even if he lived and talked. No one would believe that a tramp could meet a man like me, let alone conspire with him. Still, it is well to be cautious. I kept my straw fedora from Bergdorf well down on my face, murmured to him about his prospects, gave nothing away.

Not that my young friend asked about me. He jabbered excitedly about himself. Most of it was gibberish, but I gathered that was homeless in the literal sense of the word, not the way that word is used by social workers to cover flophouses or subsidized rentals. He had been sleeping in Battery Park. His family up in Québec had washed its hands of him. His name was Julien. He was friendless. He had no role in the world. He was simply my prophet, and altogether perfect.

After this late lunch or early supper I led him to a certain cheap hotel I know on Charles Lane, a corner of Greenwich Village too dark to be gentrified. It is a place meant for the cheapest of cheap assignations. I gave Julien cigarettes, and more money than he could have seen since Montréal days. I lurked in the stinking lobby while he obeyed my instructions: he demanded two keys from the desk clerk, a patient despairing black woman of seventy, obviously used to guests who gibbered. She handed over the keys without demur, without looking up from her Bible. The tramp slipped one of them to me. I sent him to his room, ordered him to bed, promised him a visit in the morning.

It had all gone neatly. But just before he went upstairs he tried to kiss my hand and it struck me that I might have overdone my kindness. The luxury of sheets, curtains, a roof, might recall him to his rightful mind. I didn't want that. Thank God there's always demon drink to keep wanderers in the broad path of madness. I presented Julien with my hipflask of brandy as a final benison and slipped away.

That evening, when the heat was supportable, I drove out to New Jersey, to the skidrow called Elizabeth, and found a goodwill store. I was amazed at its interesting old clothes. There were racks and racks of well-made jackets, a little out at the elbow and patched with leather, but the more authentic for that. In one happy half hour I had assembled a small wardrobe for what I usually spend on a pair of socks. I brought a ratty old suitcase to hold it all and went home happy.

Next morning I returned to the Charles Lane dive in a cab. My *protégé* was still abed. His room stank of expensive cognac and cheap vomit and bum, that is, of him. I had him shower and shave and try on his new clothes. Another miracle: Julien looked more-or-less decent. I took him out to breakfast and no one glanced at us. We might have been anyone: a patrician uncle, say, keeping an eye on a nephew who was slumming mildly on the Lower East Side. As a piece of social work, the cleaned-up Julien was a triumph. Which calls to mind an oddity of the North American class system. While no one could never make a podgy *bourgeois* pass as one of the elect, scrawny hobos do rather well. Their skinniness is ambiguous, so are their reptilian eyes. So is their tension.

I spent hours and hours with Julien over the next weeks, smoothing but never soothing. He learned or recovered some decency of manner. He held his cigarette at a plausibly nervous angle. His drunkenness took on dash. By the end of that fortnight I had created a workable *pastiche* of a certain type of intense, tormented preppie.

An artist is an artisan who knows when to stop. A few more days might have ruined – that is, unruined – Julien. He was getting within howling distance of sanity. Only the liquor I fed him morning and night kept his mind "open," as he put it, "to God's screams." I had made his exterior impressively shabby genteel while preserving his soul unspoilt, a whistling weathercock.

He was ready. He had the sheen of polish, yet he was still a passive jagged stone, my munition of rock, ready to hurl at Scuffy.

Section (5).

Now where was the target, you may ask, at that butt end of July?

Was Scuffy in my country place on Champaign, iniquitously ceded her by the court? No: having achieved that victory she'd left my children at the lake with the beatnik nanny and vanished.

So was she back in her *pied-à-terre* on Mulholland Drive, overlooking a swimming-pool brown and slimy with gigolos, with a billion dollar view of the Los Angeles smog? Eh? Was she submerged in that remote putrescence?

No she was not. She was were she had no right to be. It stings me to speak of it.

The Bertrams have always been, since we achieved affluence and cast off yokel Methodism, Episcopalian. And not just Episcopalian. We have been good Episcopalians. Physically we remained fixed in Greenwich Village or thereabouts: back when it was still a proper village with a duckpond, two miles north of the city wall; hanging on through the days of hippies and yippies and decay; glorying in its revival. But spiritually we followed the vogue in churches. In life we were churchwardens and pillars of, successively,

Grace, Trinity, Barnabas and Polycarp-in-the-Village, as the fashion for parishes, as for everything else, moved Uptown then Down again. And in death we transmogrified ourselves into expensive stained glass or memorial slaps of porphyry. My grandmother lives on as half the Cathedral organ. Uncle Caspar is a lead bas-relief in St Barnabas of the Holy Innocents. I myself intended to die into holy tablehood. The Rector of St. Polycarp craves a new gilded altar, I had intended I would be it.

No longer. Scuffy's divorce proceedings were a revelation. *The Church sided with her against me*, inflicting a shock of betrayal worse even than Drewster & May's.

Scuffy, born as she was in the purple of Hollywood, grew up an intractable muddle. Astrology, mystic feminism, nature-worship and what she called Tibetan Buddhism oozed over each other in her mind, if we are going to use that noun. Naturally she liked lava-lamps. A glob of lukewarm colored grease rises lazily to the top; at once it cools, disintegrating as it drifts down through glycerol of contrasting colors. Her globs were harmless nonsense, they required no one's attention. So you would think. Yet those damned Episcopalian clerics attended.

What did they have to do with her? It was Momsie's doing. Momsie decreed that Scuffy must be baptized and confirmed before I could have her. The film industry stink was to be hosed off with holy water. Scuffy was duly instructed, doused, ritually fondled by a bishop. We were married as he-Episcopalian and plausible-enough she-Episcopalian.

The happy event was perpetrated in St. Polycarp's, built by my great-grandfather for the poor, as there then were, of Greenwich Village. His conscience had grown queasy over child labor in his factories. He laid on a Tiffany rose-window (*Suffer the little ones to come unto Me*) and his conscience was soothed. Scuffy, passing numbly down the aisle lit by that stained-glass, balancing a lily-of-the-valley on the family Prayer Book, nearly looked like one of us. Her yellow tan, for instance, had faded to something less racially ambiguous. Her dragging gait, which is how she got her nickname, might be understood as languor and not mere idiocy. Momsie rested a positively gracious smile on her. My aunts in the second pew could not disapprove nearly as much as they hoped. Things might, they whispered (managing not to glance back at cousin-by-marriage Leah) have been worse.

Well, then: Scuffy had been Episcopalianized, made presentable. Who'd have thought she'd be impudent enough to try to enter into the *spirit* of the thing?

There is an Italian *palazzo* in Greenwich Village, literally a palace from Italy, standing not far from the Bertrams' own bought-and-paid-for church of Polycarp's.

In the 1890s a certain dizzy Vanderbilt heiress, a relation of ours, scooped up the goods in Europe: here a Tuscan library, there an Umbrian ceiling, paintings from Naples, gloomy woodwork from Rome, tapestries from some broken-down bishops' lair in the Tyrol, bits of marble façade, scraps of parquetry. She shipped the lot over and assembled it as a giant-sized playhouse to please her handsome little wop of a husband, a dentist's son named Bocchi, Bacchi or Bicchi.

Faith to move mountains is a slight thing, mountains being formless and inert. Cousin Elaine might easily have consoled Bocchi with an Apennine. Instead she flew over a whole slab of European civilisation, which landed with every carved panel in its proper place, majolica vases upright on mantels.

Its presence in Greenwich Village has always been insane. Even when it first arrived it must have seemed quaint, plonked down amidst the mellow colonial houses then facing Abingdon Square, named for dear old Willoughby Bertie, Earl of Abingdon, another connection of us Bertrams as it happens. The eighteenth-century faded slowly in Abingdon Square. But it has thoroughly faded now. The aristocratic townhouses have been blotted out by bleak apartment buildings, with only Elaine's *palazzo* surviving on the north-west corner of the square, peering shortsightedly at flowering trees and a particularly bloodthirsty statue of a doughboy. It looks, now, positively unearthly, beamed in by sportive flying saucers. But in fact sex is the uncanny force that beamed it down. Sex, or perhaps faith in the possibility of sexual fidelity.

Which is folly. By the early 'Twenties Bocchi had tired of antiques, ceramic and human. He left his Vanderbilt heiress for a teenage meatpacker or was it a saloon-girl? And she, the heiress, broken-hearted, pined and prayed and died, leaving her impossible mansion (with a lump sum for maintenance) to the Episcopalian Church.

Fill in the dates, Blundell, Blundell. Check the names. This section had better be accurate, since we are describing the site, I affirm, I assert, of the homicide.

Clergymen, I find, are paradoxical creatures, cunning and simple both. I'm sure they played Mrs. Bocchi along nicely: here a pointed sermon, there some soothing flattery from the archdeacon, here a perfectly modulated sigh. In the end they got the will they wanted, or nearly. No doubt they'd have preferred to own the house outright, so they could sell. Mrs. Bocchi wasn't having that. She set the place up as a spiritual trust, to be what is called a retreat house, and requested it be named The House of Celestial Comfort. The Bishop of New York kept a straight face and accepted the bequest.

So there it stands, on Abingdon Square: all preposterous loggias, pediments, standing globes, lion-foot tables. Ironwork nymphs writhe up and down the banisters. Cleverly-carved satyrs leer out at you from every mahogany bedpost. You can't rest you hand below a newel-post without discovering a hard nipple of teak. The House of Celestial Comfort doesn't strike me as a settling place to make peace with ones Maker. But then that has never been one of my ambitions.

However, God was one of Scuffy's ambitions, or so it seemed. The Episcopalian glob remained uppermost in her lava-lamp brain. Soon after our marriage she started frequenting Celestial Comfort. She liked going to that palatial clubhouse midweek, whenever we in town, to have her soul buffed and waxed. Then she'd come back to me and babble about spirituality, which is I gather is much like Spiritualism only respectable, and infinitely duller.

You'd think New York would smile at Scuffy's piety, taking it for the pretentious foible of an *arriviste*. Which is exactly what it was. Yet our own clerical caste, so crafty with Mrs. Bocchi, a rich Manhattan wife who could after all tell Mannerist masters from daubs, were amazingly credulous about Mrs. Bertram, a rich Manhattan wife who could scarcely read a clock. This is what I mean about the paradox of priestcraft. Clergymen are sly as snakes. Yet they also coo and flutter like pigeons. I do not understand it.

I understood Scuffy all too well. She was of good family as family is understood in movieland. Long ago her grandfather was cheated out of a fortune by one of the Ms in M.G.M. Or somesuch. One of her father's wives was once married to a Rossellini – is that right? An ex-step-uncle is something in French Art House cinema. I can't be expected to remember details. Of course she was money, but the Los Angeles sort, not the same commodity as ours. Ours falls steadily as New England drizzle. Theirs comes down in monsoons and burns away like jungle mist. Her prominence of that order. There was nothing *to* her. Grasp her hooters and frankly you grasped all there was. But the clergy, our clergy, our own ancestral allies and retainers at Celestial Comfort, affected to take her seriously, not as a Bertram spouse but as a *soul*. I resent this very much.

I resented their attitude even more when our marriage, such as it was, broke asunder last winter, and Scuffy was allowed to take "refuge" at the *palazzo*. 'Refuge'! You'd think, from the way the clergymen put it, or the way she put it herself while being deposed, that I'd flung her shoeless into the snow of Gramercy Park, that she'd groped her way cross-town through a blizzard, blinded by tears. In fact she came in a cab, and within a day or two had caused some of the best furniture from my house to be moved to that nest of priestlings. They gave her a suite of rooms, and she spent her six months there in the guise of a luxurious informal nun, going to pseudo-monastic offices in the ballroom-chapel, conversing intensely about whatever religious people discuss, airily hawking cakes at church *fêtes*. She was often sighted lunching alone at Babbo or Blue Hill, reading a book of devotion while picking at sixty-dollar baked potatoes. Oh yes, Manhattan Society was enormously edified by Scuffy. Greenwich Village wondered if it had produced its first saint.

Even the advent of that semi-musical gangster didn't dent her new reputation. She loved the depraved rapper Kelt-Doggie? Why then, she had assimilated the Sermon on the Mount. She was lubricating the detritus of the earth. She was building the kingdom of God amongst us! I was alienated. The whole isle is my native beat, from its serene Georgian brick façades at the bottom, through mile-high glass towers, to blobby chocolate brownstones even further Uptown. Hushed white-dressed restaurants, gross yellow cabs flying up and down the avenues, up and down, cocktail parties in apartments in the sky, each sporting an acre of plate-glass full of summer-dusk Central Park: this is all properly mine. New York is my ground of prey. Now the city bore the spore of Scuffy. I'd overhear gossip: "She manned a charity beauty-salon for the homeless?" "In a church basement! On *Staten Island*." She brought Doggie to an orphanage to perform his masterwork *Fuck me up jiggy bitch* to adoring waifs, then made him sign autographs on their foreheads with her Shiseido lipstick. She herself saved the rain-forest by standing singing *Kumbaya* in the drizzle, under an umbrella held by a smirking parson, holding hands with similarly afflicted persons, in front of the Brazilian consulate. "Well, I'll be ...." Families who'd known the Bertrams for generations began to watch me askance: "Was it not you who drove forth the holy one?"

Decency would have kept me away from Scuffy and her preposterous palace-monastery. You indecent ones, Blundell, Blundell, Hobbel and Kringe, yes I mean you, felt no such scruple. We had just lost the first round of our legal tussle with Scuffy. You insisted I go through the forms of seeking reconciliation with the bitch. The New York County Family Court smiles on husbands who try to recover their wives and fail.

Therefore on July 17th I presented myself in Abingdon Square, armed with a bouquet, while you, Mr. Hobbel, lurked in a van on the bosky corner of Bethune Street, along with a discreet photographer. (Include the photographs at this point. They cost me enough.)

How shameful to appear at that door as a suppliant! I have attended my share of thousand-dollar-a-plate fundraisers at the House of Celestial Comfort. I expect to be bowed in as a donor. No, I was admitted with a certain tender reproachfulness, horribly Christian. Then they kept me pacing about a barren vaulted waiting-room. Every so often a religious person peered round the big carved doors, his face full of

> *Christian, dost thou see them, on the holy ground,*
> *How the troops of Midian prowl and prowl around?*

That was my favorite hymn at Groton. I did not relish being demoted to the Midianite class.

I saw how this farce must end. Scuffy would refuse to see me. I would prowl away. And so she did. But instead of being merely chucked out, I was led into the presence of a much-too-smooth Britisher in a clerical collar, and invited to take a seat, or rather a madly-inlaid Renaissance faldstool on which I must have looked silly.

I took his Britishness in my stride. The Bertram family is not in awe of the Old World. We are, or have become, descendants of a cadet branch of the Viscounts Nansough. We might if we wanted have come over with the Conqueror – or emigrated to Babylon from the Garden of Eden. In cold historic fact we made our first pile victualling the Redcoats. General Howe was extremely polite to great-great-great-great-grandfather, who was feeding his men on credit. Each subsequent generation of Bertram felt quite at home over There. We'd swagger off clipper, paddler, steamer or jet and set to work patronizing the Old Country. Great-grandmother, after she discovered from a drunken footman the Awful Truth about great-grandfather, retired across the Atlantic altogether, and spent her last decades as a fixture of Mayfair. Even Momsie, in old age, after her Jungian-alienist period in Switzerland, found a stray Hungarian prince to marry, and briefly cut a dash in the circle of the mad bad Princess of Wales. I realize *all* Americans seem funny to a certain sort of Britisher. But I can out-British any of them. Leverage, leverage, that's what it comes down to. So why did this one dismay me?

"For Scuffy," I snapped, handing him my flowers. This failed to wipe the damned urbane smile off his face.

"I'll give them to your wife, Mr. Bertram," he said, laying them appraisingly across one forearm, then putting them aside on a *pietra dura* table. "But she asks me to tell you she won't see you; understandably – "

"And who are you, passing on such a message?'

I couldn't shake the smile. "Just someone staying here." He did not volunteer a name. "She is well.'

"I'm sorry to hear it."

I should not have gone so far. He'd riled me. Those eyes, not smiling although the mouth kept up its curve, rested for a moment in mine. "A murderous remark," he said absolutely seriously, still lip-smiling. Only then did he turn me into the street like a panhandler.

I record this scrap of conversation because I'm convinced that there are certain human beings who know about blood. It's an absolute divide. On one side are the herd: people like you, you pitiful attorneys, feebly trying to do good because you're so afraid of evil, and failing. On this side those of us who are not afraid and do not fail. There are a fair number of us on Wall Street who have done ordered done what needed to be done during our careers, and are crowned with the mark of Cain. "A murderous remark:" I saw I had been recognized. But I could only be recognized by a brother, who had therefore betrayed himself. The presence of such a one in such a place disquieted me.

You looked so very hapless, Hobbel, when I got back into the van, snarling "She wouldn't see me," because you *are* hapless. At least the photographer knew his business. He had snapped me standing outside the House of Celestial Comfort with my overpriced flowers, an honest fellow doing his darndest to win back the woman he had always loved etcetera. That picture might be worth something in court. But it was the final shots that interested me.

"Did you get that priest fellow?" The photographer nodded. You, Hobbel, looked dazed. "Find out who he is."

In your usual way you dawdled, and it was days before you got back to me to say the man was called Culpepper and wasn't a cleric at all, although he sometimes goes about disguised as one when wrecking and ruining. He is in fact a Latin professor at some Cambridge college I had not heard of, no doubt because it is right not to have heard of it. An imposter of some sort, then, and a spy. That was the sort of person my wife was consorting with in her looted palace. They must be up to something. Interesting stuff. Data, I thought, for the judge.

But this was already July 25th. Knowledge came too late. We were all in the starting-gate.

Section (6).

So we've reached the start. Do legal documents take so long to get going? I had been obliged to sue for custody, I cannot imagine why. How is it not self-evident that Chaddles, which is to say legally-speaking L. Heathrop Bertram VI, should stay in the keeping of L. Heathrop Bertram V, me? What does the numbering mean if it doesn't mean he is mine? I had proposed we divide the chattels, Scuffy to take Po. She preferred to fight it out, double or quits. I got to fight with you clowns, Scuffy with Drewster & May, which led to the *débâcle* you will have described in section (1): defeat after defeat, with more catastrophes looming as to alimony. And then the gods, see section (2), sent me my prodigy, whom I readied, sections (3-6); so much for setting.

Section (7).

Before we plunge into my great deed, I want to picture the three of us in our beds early on the night of July 26ᵗʰ.

Me first. Me, the aggrieved husband, humiliated in the courts, about to be deprived of his only son. I might properly have been consoling myself with a scarlet woman. Yet how do we find me on this final evening? Sitting up in my library, reading the Book of Ezekiel.

I don't want to give the impression that my transaction with Julien was one-sided. If I slapped social veneer on him, he introduced me to Ezekiel, that compendium of demented retribution. "I will judge thee, as women that break wedlock and shed blood are judged. I will give thee blood in fury and jealousy." I suppose every book contains horrors if horrors are what you're looking for. But the horrors of Ezekiel throw themselves on the reader. He's so lurid you think he must be joking or concocting an allegory. No: he wants to be taken straight. Ezekiel is infinitely serious, which is to say insane. I think his mind must have been much like Julien's. He has the true rhythm of violence, intoxication, the voice in the head goading to carnage. I feel asleep thinking: Ezekiel is ludicrous and entirely real. "They shall also bring up a company against thee, and they shall stone thee with stones. So I will be quiet, and will be no more angry."

Speaking of which, let's glance sneeringly at Scuffy, asleep in her preposterous velvet-curtained four-poster at the House of Celestial Comfort. She always slept naked, Scuffy, smelling of expensive wicked Californian perfumes and biting her puffy lips as she dreamed. "I will be quiet."

The prophet, in his Charles Lane dive: does he dream of blood? Does he lie awake or drink from the bottle and rant? Or – just you wait.

Oh yes: Chaddles. And Po. I hope they're enjoying nice dreams up in my Vermont lake-house, about getting ice-cream from me let us say, or being taken out on the speedboat. "And since you have custody," I told the ghost of Scuffy in my double-bed, putting away Ezekiel and turning off the lights, "if Chaddles drowns I'll be able to harrow you through every court in the forty-eight contiguous states until I have the last scrap of browned, massaged flesh off your excellent bones. *Bonne nuit.*"

Section (8).

I can always rise at the hour I chose the night before. I woke early on July 27th, day appointed for execution of my plan, and found the plan had grown splendidly ornate while I slept. Rather, it had changed from an efficient piece of brokerage into a work of art.

My basic strategy must be obvious. I'd been softening Julien up. The God of Ezekiel had a great work in store for His prophet. I'd hinted at cleansing the city of unrighteousness. The heavens were giving me, too, tidings of his mission.

This went down well. All visionaries are lonely. Solitude makes them hard and strong: it's added proof, they're persecuted for truth's sake. But they don't necessarily enjoy their loneliness. If someone joins them in delusion they weep with gladness. Julien was intoxicated by my faith in his prophetic office, and entirely pliable. If I woke him with tidings of the wickedest woman in the world, staying on Abingdon Square, whom he must cut off in the strength of the Lord before slaying himself, I was fairly certain he'd believe me. In his gentlemanly thrift-store clothes he'd pass muster at the House of Celestial Comfort. They'd let him in. He'd find her. Madmen always know how to cut a throat, I don't know why. The sane have only the vaguest idea. I was less sure about afterward. Suicides are bungled more often than murders. I didn't like the idea of Julien's surviving to be grilled. I wanted him to be for me as ice-darts were for Bopsy, vanishing, leaving nothing to link me to the corpse. He was a gentle soul who'd loathe the shouting, kicking, bright lights. I didn't want him breaking down and telling the police that a distinguished old fellow had urged him to kill Scuffy Bertram. Of course he had no idea who I was. But even policemen sometimes add two and two.

It would be nice, then, to muddy his confession so that, if he lived to make it, it wouldn't, couldn't, be credited. I wanted everything he said ignored. I wanted him hustled into a hospital for the criminally insane, with three meals a day and a well-made bed for the rest of his tolerable life. And overnight it had occurred to me how this might be done.

I'd studied the clerical abuse crisis of last decade. They were crafty operators, those pederastic priests. One trick was to do something childish before assaulting a boy – donning a Mickey Mouse mask, say – so that the victim's report would sound like make-believe. Childishness is what gives crimes against children their air of unreality. Unreality makes them safe. Or if you like: the horror of these unreal events is that they're in fact real, as Ezekiel is cartoonish, but in perfect earnest.

This idea had seeped through my mind as I slept. When I woke I went straight to the nursery.

It was empty, empty not only of the property withheld from me by the New York City Family Court, but empty of Florence and the other two. They would not arrive and begin their grisly charade of not-looking-after my no-children until ten. I had it to myself.

Every nursery is rich in terrors if terrors are what you're looking for. It was still very early. Somehow I didn't want to turn on the lights. As I groped about, battery-driven toys came to life, whimpering or snickering. Freakish human animals lolled against me come-on-ishly from the shelves. I trod over the naked legs of dolls with smiles much like Scuffy's. I kicked aside a drummer rabbit and resurrected him: he landed on his face and begin frenzied humping, heaving himself off the floor with his sticks. I had to stamp on him twice before he'd stop.

What I wanted was costuming, costuming of a certain sort. Unfortunately my children seemed to have wholesome taste, which was useless to me. There was a whole armory of long-swords and spears and spiked shields and horned helmets. (Chaddles, I recall, went through a Viking period.) There were astronaut helmets, dragon-heads, a two-child four-legged horse. There were tutus, ball-dresses, saccharine baby-animal masks, Po's, I assume. There were get-ups to turn my boy into a pirate, a bandit, a vampire, a cow-rustler, all good preparation for the serious criminality of putting on a tie and being a banker. None of it was quite right.

I meditated on the terrors of my own infancy. I'd not been a timid child. Still, I remembered a dread of certain imaginary creatures. Elves and giants were all right, but I couldn't abide mixtures: mermaids, harpies, chimæras. What of the catoblepas, with its ox body, crocodile scales, wild boar's head? Or the opinicus: long camel-neck culminating in eagle-head, four lion legs, short camel tail? Or the gryphon, much the same but hold the camel and let the front legs stay eaglish? I think I must have been given an illustrated book of classical Greek monsters when very small. I don't remember the book, but these hybrids are so vividly with me there must have been one. I could still spot a hippogriff in a police line-up.

Such monsters distressed me, perhaps, because they are not

mere muddles. They're *almost* arbitrary. They possess the almost-arbitrariness of newly-invented salads or cocktails. Some mixtures wouldn't work. A lion head on a penguin is silly or funny, nothing else. But after all, black swans and cassowaries and platypuses exist in the Antipodes, and if the world were just a fraction odder than it is, there might indeed be breeding populations of centaurs and werewolves. The ungainliness of such fancies is only a little beyond. The sphinx strains our imagination, she doesn't defy it. She stretches fancy, she makes the faculty ache. She softens it up for evil promptings. Wasn't it a sphinx who gave Œdipus his start in life? Anyway, there are fine four-faced half-human Living Beasts in Ezekiel; Julien would find a mixed monster plausible.

I set about assembling one. I could be a centaur, perhaps, using the back half of the pantomime horse. But I didn't want Julien to see my face and, to be frank, at sixty-five I haven't got quite the heroic torso I possessed in the twentieth century.

I fossicked about in my children's drawers and shelves and baskets, and at last came across a great mass of artificial feathers, which I vaguely remembered .... Of course, our drinks party in East Hampton last Thanksgiving! Chaddles had been a Puritan with a plastic axe, Po had been his turkey on a rope. This get-up was my idea. Florence got the children out of bed, dressed them, and brought them downstairs to show off to our guests. Po blubbered, fearing she was going to be dinner. Scuffy, whose medication had recently been readjusted, sobbed too, mawkishly, at how beautiful our offspring were. She smeared cranberry relish on the lapel of my tuxedo, "Where your heart ought to be." I took Chaddles' axe to threaten her with, playfully. Happy days.

Now I tore off the turkey's head, with its obscene rubber wattles, and found that the plumage, fluffed and stretched, could go round my waist. I had the makings of a hippalectryon!

You, dreary law-clerks, will think a horse-headed rooster comic. You're not picturing it properly. No doubt you didn't have my childhood advantages. No rich godfathers gave you lavish books of Greek fables. Understand: the hippalectryon in my head is simply terrific. It's a rainbow-colored bird immense as an emu, with spurred feet to put you in mind of dinosaur feet, and a sinewy breast ending, as somehow it must, in a mad red-eyed stallion, whinnying, exultant, deranged at the thought of itself. Did Greek warriors ride hippalectryons into battle? My picture-book must have shown them doing just that. That is what I see now when I close my eyes.

It was still dark when I got the car out. It was barely twilight when I got to Charles Lane. Reaching Julien before he woke was not hard, the boy kept shocking hours. The fat black lady, very jaded indeed, did not even look up as I went past with my black rubbish sack. Outside Julien's room, feeling silly as well as unrighteousness and powerful, I got out my feathered bottom, my horse head, and donned them. Terrible in strangeness, I produced my room-key from somewhere beneath the plastic ruff holding up my tail-plumes.

"Cockadoodle-neigh!" This doesn't sound serious because it is grotesque. But in this cosmos, taste is a guide to nothing at all. Wickedness spirals not just downward but outward. Our deeds get not only blacker and blacker but more and more *outré*. The world acquires the severity of hell with the inconsequence of the nightmares you see when you have a temperature of 102. People like Scuffy, who take *Vogue* as scripture, try to hold off the maelstrom of evil with sheets of pretty paper, fashion, beauty, discernment. That's all make-believe. Reality breaks in, peering at us with silly faces, just as I peered at Julien entering his room at dawn in the toy-store kitsch from Taiwan with which, in perfect earnest, I slew my wife.

Section (9).

Is there an absolute legal rule against dreams being entered as evidence? I don't care. It's my affidavit, I'm paying for it, I'll write what I like. Section (9) concerns spectral events endured the evening of the day Julien was addressed by a hippalectryon.

I was exhausted. I was exhausted with relief at his terror. I was exhausted with his ecstasy at getting definite orders at last. His emotions were correct. They were all I could desire.

I was also exhausted from the long solitary lunch at the Princeton Club with which I'd celebrated my coming victory, or rather my present victory, for on Wall Street we have a saying "a sure thing suspends the rules." If you're certain something's going to come through, it stops being speculation, it's just scooping up gold daisies from a lawn. The laws of time ceases to apply. You travel through time, future triumph can be enjoyed now, you can borrow against it.

I'd told Julien to arrive the House of Celestial Comfort at cocktail hour, when Scuffy was sure to be in. Yet already at midday I could savor my widowhood. I had three I think it was martinis and two bottles of Pouilly-Vinzelles with my whatever. Acquaintances nodded at me across the dining room but kept their distance. Not that I was sodden or uncouth. But they guessed I wanted to be alone, consoling myself over my messy divorce. So they thought; really I was carousing over my tidy bereavement.

The elegance of the deed made me prouder and prouder the more I considered it. All I'd done was dress up in children's toys and frighten a mad tramp. Yet I'd fathomed the age, thwarted injustice, saved a dynasty. I'd invented an art-form: assassinating with a sonnet, with a ballet-spin. With an oboe-trill ....

After lunch I became more sociable and stood people glasses of bourbon in the club bar. When Manhattan had grown purple and fantastic enough I reeled into a taxi, which took me through the sunset East Village to Gramercy Park; I reeled out and on the third try got the door open. I performed a dance up the stairs which was unwise but I wasn't hurt at all. Florence and her minions appeared boggling but I shouted at them to go home and they went. I got my clothes off just before my head vanished into the pillow, I dreamed with confusion and bad-taste of Scuffy live and Scuffy dead, Scuffy rotting, Scuffy with me in bed. I woke a tad before midnight to find a hippalectryon sitting on my bed.

This was apparently to be one of those veridical dreams, which I'd heard of, but never endured, in which the victim can move and speak and think and even toy nervously with his sheets. "Ah," I said aloud, experimentally. Then, since my voice sounded normal: "Good evening."

The voice from inside the horse-head did not sound normal. It was like an actor affecting a bestial croak. "Julien has done our bidding."

It was no moment for tact. "Scuffy's dead, then?" The head nodded awkwardly, upward, like a real horse bothered by flies. A victorious dream, then. Courtesy within the skull. The faculty called Fancy was congratulating the faculty called Intellect. "Julien's cut her throat?"

(Part of the charm and horror of horses is that, as with humanity, the beauty lies in nudity of flesh. A cow's pelt is merely uncut leather. But in horses the veins show, and muscles move visibly though the warm smooth skin, just as with us. It's easy to imagine what a knife against the throat feels like to a horse.)

"He did," said the impossible. "He stole a knife from the kitchen and found her in the chapel."

(As the nudity of horses makes them poignant, so this monster's feathers, for all the splendid mustard and emerald and crimson, were merely animal, that is, horrid. There'd be cold bumpy reptilian skin beneath, if I dared touch – I'd rather die, I'd rather die.)

My thoughts came as I'm representing them, slowly, clumsily, randomly. It was the clumsiness that made the dream seem so real. I felt like a man woken from heavy sleep, not a man who is heavily asleep. "Did she scream?"

"No. She prayed."

(It was all nonsense, these thoughts of horseskin and roosterskin. I wasn't imagining a real hippalectryon, I was imagining a man dressed up and putting on a weird voice. Why? "Why," I self-consciously wondered, "am I giving myself such an extraordinarily self-conscious dream?" I felt the beginnings of a different sort of fear, beyond an uneasiness about uncanny creatures sitting on my bed. Rather than attend to this fear, I kept up the mad conversation.)

"And did he kill himself, as commanded?"

(A cruel inner voice alleged that I was only chatting to stop myself being frightened. But to my credit, I did care. I wanted Julien to be honorably, picturesquely dead, lying with a kitchen knife buried in his chest. Or already in a police morgue. A policeman should be drawing his outline in white chalk. I hoped he wasn't trapped in a cell raving about horsefeathers, being beaten and despised. Julien had opened up so beautifully when I took the warrant of the prophet seriously. He'd resent the verdict of insanity.)

"No," creaked the voice from beneath the rubber horse-mask. "He did not kill himself. Just knelt over the body, swaying back and forth. That's what he was doing when the sacristan came in. To light candles for compline."

"Did *he* scream?"

"No. He locked the door and went to find … that English clergyman you met ten days ago. Pseudo-clergyman, it's only a travelling disguise. His real specialty is dealing with this sort of thing. Killing and so forth."

(I didn't like the sound of this. Although I knew all this was happening in my head, even the pretence of Culpepper's getting involved was troubling. Nor did I like this loose talk of criminal specialties.)

"And the pseudo-vicar came in to Julien and talked to him. In English by the way. Parisian French troubles Julien, who naturally speaks the thickest Québécois."

"... Naturally."

"Julien told him about being rescued from the streets. By a kind, kind, beautifully-dressed man. About being given lots to eat and put in a fine room. Then ordered to murder by a 'horse-faced chicken.'"

"He's mad."

"That's why he might have been used. The longer he talked the more useful his lunacy sounded. It wasn't hard to guess who the kind old man might be. But what about the hippalectryon? Not that Julien had heard of hippalectryons. Us gigichooks. Us ancient Greek critters. But the pseudo-vicar knew the name. He recognized us from Julien's description."

Crazy thinking is thinking too. "This," I told the monster with appalling calm, "is the worse nightmare I've ever had. Or heard of."

An immensely loud: "Nei-hei-hei-heigh!" from under the horse-head. Then an entirely different voice, British, educated, not the stagey croak: "I hoped you'd say that."

With another shake – side to side, not like a horse's shake, like a man's – the head came loose. Human hands came up and took it and pulled it off the neck.

We were in classic nightmare territory at last, decapitation, nonsense, metamorphosis, familiar horrors. But things did not go in that direction at all. There I was staring, so it seemed, into the smug intelligent face of the false Culpepper, who was holding a large rubber horse-head in his lap.

"Dr Culpepper!" I said.

The face frowned. "You know my name?" The frown lightened: "Why shouldn't you? You're clever enough, it's a privilege to unmask you. Why shouldn't you unmask me? Speaking of which, do you mind if I shed it all?"

He stood and started climbing out of his luxurious disguise while I shut my eyes and made a fierce effort to wake up. When I opened them he was reverently laying his many-colored feathered body-sheath across a chair. Orange feathers below the head modulated to yellow over the neck; layers of crimson, teal and dark orange glorified the flanks. The tail was a tremendous upward cascade of amethyst. I had not been so beautiful.

It seemed best to remain suave and not scream. "Might I compliment you on your plumage," I murmured, "hippalectryon to hippalectryon?"

"Hip hip hooray." Culpepper was sitting now to remove his yellow stockings, on a bedroom chair not my bed. "No, thank you sincerely. You know, Manhattan must be the only place on earth where you can get party costumes in the wee hours. I stopped on the way at an all-year, open-all-night Halloween store. On Jane Street. Also, Greenwich Village must be the only *quartier* where a man can drive about like this in an open Jeep and not be noticed. The breed's Brown Leghorn they told me. Isn't it beautiful? I was sorry to have to leave off the comb. Twelve inches tall. Cherry-red. Frankly, I wasn't so pleased within *this*." He laid on top of the rooster-costume the horse-head, which was a demoniacally-eyed nag, a Halloween bogey. "A bit coarse. Ah well." Underneath his nonsense Culpepper wore tight black pants and a black silk T-shirt. He looked like a cat-burglar or a film producer. He smoothed his hair and gazed at me quizzically; not an entirely unfriendly look. "I think we still have a few minutes. Shall we chat?"

"What," I said at random, "has happened to Julien?"

"I left him locked in the basement. In that mad *palazzo* on Abingdon Square. And drove cross-town in my Jeep. To test my theory. Which is well and truly tested now. You've said everything I could have wanted."

I reminded myself it was a dream, still a dream. Nonetheless I folded my arms, refusing to incriminate myself further. I was not Bopsy. No Erkhaerdt was going to bounce me into confessing an insoluble murder.

"Don't sulk, Bertram. Sulking's unworthy of us. You and I may be the least-deceived men on the planet. Besides it's too late. Let's be nice to each other before we go our separate ways." I raised a scornful eyebrow. This phantom was insolent. "Listen. Some time ago I made an immense discovery." I was indifferent. I heard him out. "A modern doesn't think with his intellect but with his imagination – an imagination deadened by being force-fed imagery. He thinks in pictorial clichés, utterly incapable of abstraction. This is why he can't credit rational religion: he pictures God in a nightie on a cloud and sniggers. It's why he *can* credit the advertisements. He's shown a sugary drink juxtaposed on tanned bodies, it makes *pictorial* sense, he's persuaded." I feigned boredom. Incredible that even a dream-professor barely emerged from a chicken-suit, sitting in a murderer's bedroom, should be so professorial. "People imagine any idea that's unimaginable must be false. Why? It's a surprising world. Why shouldn't the visually absurd be true?"

I wasn't paying much attention to Culpepper's discourse and may not be doing justice to it. I was trying to decide whether, even in a dream, I dared get out of bed and look through my drawers for Delano, my teddy-bear.

"I assumed," he went on, prim, feline, opaque, "that I was the only person alive who knew this great secret, *and applied it*. I can hide any deed simply by making it too grotesque to picture. I'm master of the world." Delano made me go to sleep in the 'Fifties. Would he still work? "Then earlier this evening Julien confessed to me. I realized that there must be another master loose in New York. A lesser master no doubt, a poor man's me. Still, it was a shock."

I patronizingly patted his hand. A mistake. The hand felt as warm as a real hand. I was suddenly more unhappy. Rather than whimper, I pouted. "I *hadn't* theorized all this," I told the apparition, "I never theorize. I just have a knack for deceiving people." I seemed to be underselling myself. "I'm regarded with terror on Wall Street."

"You're an *idiot savant* then! Well, that doesn't diminish your genius." Was it a good sign or not that I was feeling so tired? Is anyone tired in a dream? "What a genius of a crime! I don't mean using a demented vagrant. New York's awash with them, nothing's easier than inducing one to kill, anyone might do that. But only a master would know to drape his act in myth. You knew no policeman or lawyer can believe the fantastic, not because it's improbable but because it's fantastic. You used the great secret. You should have been safe." Towards the end of this speech doubts started growing on me, I mean doubts of my doubts. They became intense when Culpepper impudently laid his hands on my shoulder. "How unfair that you should run into the only man less deceived than yourself!"

The plausible weight of that hand was dreadful. "Off," I said, unsuavely, "ludicrous phantasm. You're not here."

"Now you're making the exact mistake you want the police to

make. My presence is ludicrous but that doesn't make me untrue, does it? – I hear shouting." There did seem to be a *fracas* in the street. Culpepper began to speak more urgently. "I think I'd better present you with this."

In a daze I reached out for his gift. He put into my hand in an ordinary kitchen-knife: he held the blade, using a handkerchief, I numbly took the handle. "What is it?"

"You know what it is. Listen," and what followed came in an insane rush: "I drove across from the House of Celestial Comfort with Mrs. Bertram in the back covered in rubbish bags and she's now lying in the front garden of this house, her white face prone to catch street-light glare since her bleeding's stopped blood being pretty much gone. If you'd been innocent and not recognized a hippalectryon I'd have retrieved her at once, taken her back and let Julien take what you people call the rap. But not so not and now some passer-by has evidently spotted her and is raising the alarm. I'm about to slip out that window carrying all this party paraphernalia, drive back to Abingdon Square, collect Julien, take him to Penn Station to put on a sleeper to Montréal – he doesn't have a passport so Mounties will engulf him if it's still Mounties who guard the Canadian frontier, he should be back with his family in a few days so your tool won't suffer and I hope that makes you happy. You're too old and complaisant to climb out the window with me and are going to prison forever, goodbye."

"I," I said, with heroic, defiant calm, "am asleep. This over-elaborate dream is merely the revenge of my conscience. Bolstered by overmuch white burgundy at lunch. Your presence in my dream, Culpepper, is evidence that I dread your knowing eye. That's all. I don't know if Julien's done what he was told. I don't care. I'm safe. It was the perfect murder if it happened. Bobsy's surpassed. I'm going back to sleep now."

The black figure had long since vanished out the window. I was speaking to the air. But then the whole thing had been addressed to myself. I was alone in the Manhattan night, as usual. Outside were the usual Manhattan noises: honks, lovers shouting at each other as they walked home, cat-fights, sirens. The sirens seemed to be getting closer, but that's always the way in Manhattan. It is always best to ignore the outside. I dropped the imaginary knife on my actual bedside table, lay down and composed myself to sleep. I was sure

I was still dreaming when I heard the doorbell, masculine shouts, warnings. I lay still while the police seemed to be kicking in my door. A sudden rush of uniforms into my bedroom, lights in my eyes, apparent flourishing of guns: I outfaced all that, I clung to delusive sanity through it all. It was only the rasp of handcuff on wrist, a new, peculiar sensation, that won me over.

Section (10).

Outhippalectryonized!

This is what outraged and outrages me. What would we say if the gods raised a sudden wave, tremendous enough to devour a city, only to open a mysterious crevice in the seafloor and swallow it before anyone noticed? We'd call it be a fidget. We'd call it insanely profligate.

My prophet came to me as a pure gift from the realm of random magic. Where's the sense in providing a miracle then trumping it with a slightly greater miracle?

Take a broader view. Why breed up a master cynic with (let us say) 1000% of the usual human capacity for incredulity and deceit, just to smash against him another cynic with 1020%?

What is the joke of which I am the butt? How, precisely, are the prodigal gods amused? Shouldn't I be told?

Section (11).

I am not childish enough to tax the New York Police Department with the same disloyalty I object to in priests and lawyers. For eight generations my family has systematically corrupted this city's Force. The cops did not forget it, and dealt with me far more tenderly than they would have dealt with Julien. They were positively polite, once the handcuffs were on and their coward hearts stopped thudding.

The same could not be said of the gutter journalists already assembled in Gramercy Park, hyena-pack-wise, to photograph me as I was helped into a patrol car and driven away.

The next morning I was arraigned –

But no. I am not going to bother finishing section (11). You, Blundell, Blundell can do it for me, summarizing my legal toils in the grisly *argot* of your trade. It's your trade, not mine. I have watched the courtroom games with detachment. I do not propose to pay my stake when I lose.

Nonetheless the spectacle has depressed me. I was always blue chip stock, bought and sold at a premium. Now I'm a junk bond. Even the District Attorney, a minor celebrity whom I helped put in place, leaves my case to his underlings.

Who have done their work well enough. I was remanded without bail on the grounds of 'flight risk'. Aren't the rich always bailed? Before that first hearing I denied to you that I had any idea of absconding, a plausible lie you ought to have been able to retail to the judge. As it happens I had a lovely scheme of flight worked out. I was going by inconspicuous 'bus to Rochester, a ragged city where I'm told they sell passports at least as good as the real thing. Then Cuba for pleasure; then Cambridge, England, for a piece of business; then the wide world.

What a waste of imagination! Through your incompetence bail was refused. Then in your defeatist way you shrugged off the fascinating question of my innocence and settled down to plea-bargaining. Thus I've been sitting in jail watching summer decay through the bars, watching a single unshapely beech begin to strip itself.

It's true that I have not, until now, told you the truth. There seemed no point. The crime of which I am unjustly accused, and sure be convicted if things reach that point, happens to be less heinous that the crime of which I am guilty.

The false contention of the People in *The State of New York v. Bertram* is that Scuffy, hoping to patch things up, returned in the middle of the night to the marital home, where I killed her with the kitchen knife later found covered with my finger-prints, and flung her down our stoop into the garden. That these are all odd acts *adds* to the weight of the State's case. "This Bertram guy was nuts, see?" It was a crime of passion. I'm to be pitied if not quite admired for my ardor.

I do not know what they would say if I could make them believe the cold-blooded thing I truly did, or even to understand it. "Y'er saying there was two hippie electrons?": imagine that in the accent of a 'tec bred on Staten Island. No, it seemed better to let things wind their inane way toward the inevitable.

Section (12).

I do not complain of this jail. It is physically more comfortable than Groton, and far more chaste. No one interferes with my solitude. Nor does anyone interfere with my small remaining stock of personal property. I have, for instance, an expensive-looking bottle of heart pills by my bunk. The Rector of St Polycarp brought it to me on one of his pastoral visits. His fine fleshy Episcopalian smile cowered the guards, who didn't examine the bottle carefully. They ought to have. The top layers are what is says on the label. The ones at the bottom, a slightly paler shade of blue, are not. I have not decided when to help myself to those illicit tablets. But it will be soon.

This detail is, of course, covered by lawyer-client privilege. Do not try to dissuade me. I do not have the patience for the farce of a full trial. Nor, I suppose, does your firm relish a shattering public defeat. Very well, let us make our bows when we're still actors in something like a drawing-room comedy, before we descend to realism, absurdity, grit.

Speaking of absurdity: I gather that there is an unofficial *cultus* of Scuffy. The House of Celestial Comfort is already cashing in. Her room is a mountain of fresh flowers. Pilgrims come. The sacerdotal tour-guides go to the limit of good taste. She was too fine for this hard world: far too fine for me, too fine even for Doggie. The pilgrims nod, bow their heads, add their flowers, then go out to gawp holily about Abingdon Square, sniffing for the ghost of pain, cadging for relics. Might she have softened her anguish in this very wine-bar? Trembles of devotion! They steal the ash-trays just in case.

These spiritual trippers are surely lowering the tone of Greenwich Village, and may already have depressed property values, as I pointed out to the Rector. He responded with a mooncalf smirk. For all I know he has commissioned an icon of St Scuffy. I therefore refuse to be buried from St Polycarp. Please do note this, legal minions.

Section (13).

To less mad matters. I set a firm of private detectives on the trail of Julien, but he was duly arrested at the border and sucked into the maw of the Canadian social services, which are extremely discreet. "Julien" seems not have been his real name. He never told me that. He was less trusting than I assumed. It pains me to think he might have doubted me. Still, I feel a certain wry affection. I trust the creepiness that beset him after we met will come to seem to him a phantasmagoria, a midsummer dream. I like to picture him years from now, walking small dogs about Montréal, shoveling snow in front of old age homes: harmless small acts of that sort. I forgive him his weakness.

Kelt-Doggie, whom I forgive nothing, will obtain ownership of Chaddles and Po. It turns out that just before her death Scuffy went through an online Buddhist rite of 'spirit-binding' with him, which the Episcopalian Church affects to take seriously. Even more shockingly, the court thinks it tantamount to marriage. Doggie will thus be guardian to two poppets about to inherit my fortune on top of Scuffy's.

He will nonetheless squander as much as he can, although the trust lawyers at Drewster & May are tenacious in a way you Blundell clowns could not understand. Anyway he is sure to bring my son up terribly. I can easily picture my boy, and his sister, dying of overdoses at seventeen.

But let's optimistically assume Chaddles survives his Hollywood childhood. This affidavit, which has no practical effect for me, may then be of use to him. There are always people to sue, estates to sue when the bodies are cold, deeds to extenuate if bodies are still warm.

Very well, then, inadequate law-mongers of Blundell. All this I affirm, assert, confess, declare under the blah-blah blah, write in heart's-blood using Momsie's exhumed and sharpened thigh-bone if that helps. Cast it into legal form, suppressing what you must, preserving though the central act. Bring it back to my cell for signing. Then consign it to your vaults. It is to lie untouched until it's brought up on the eighteenth birthday of my son Chaddles, that is, L. Heathrop Bertram VI. On September 27th 2019 it is to be brought up, de-dusted by a lawyerly puff-puff-puff, and handed to him. He is to read it in your offices if your law firm is still extant which is more than it deserves. What happens then is up to Chaddles.

And to Po, of course. Miss Portia Bertram, that is to say. Poor Po: I suppose it will have been upsetting for you to grow up thinking your father killed your mother in a moment of brutal rage. I trust it is consoling to learn he killed her in an artistic fashion. Is it? Or not? I cannot fathom females. Frankly there is a limit to how much I care.

But Chaddles *my boy*: you will understand me. Dr. Culpepper, who teaches dead languages at a dead university in the dead land of England, orphaned you. I lay on you no burden of vengeance. That would be too Gothic. I merely point him out as someone about whom you might want to think about in the abstract.

I hope you will be a chip off the old block. In which case, dear child, this may not be farewell, but merely *au revoir!*

L. Heathrop Bertram V
10/5/12

Send me Felix, Chaddles. *Send me Felix.*

II.

Hillazon,

or,

The Castaway of Venice

With him came that smell no one else seem to notice.

"They are disinfecting Venice – why?" The mountebank answered hoarsely: "Because of the police. Orders, *signore*. On account of the heat and the sirocco." "So there is no plague in Venice?" The man's expressive face fell, he put on a look of comical innocence. "A plague? What sort of plague? Is the sirocco a plague? Or perhaps our police are a plague! You are making fun of us, *signore!*"

THOMAS MANN,
Death in Venice

I think, sir, that you a minister of the Anglican Schism – if that is a polite way of putting it?

You smile, so I suppose it isn't. *Questa Inglese! Riserva loro!* Forgive me. *Madre mio.* My nanny, Mrs Vaux, was from Northumberland, a decayed recusant widow, her own words you understand; then I was educated by Irish Jesuits. There is a sectarian skew, which I deplore, to my stock of English, such as it is. –

What? Oh, too kind, sir, too kind. And I'm sure quite untruthful. I hardly ever get to speak it nowadays, except to Americans, and then …. And I fear I read your wonderful language too much, far too much. I have reached that point of life when the French novelists seem too half clever, the Russians too gloomy. Gloomsome. Gloomy. Which? I mean *cupi, raccapriccianti, triste*…. But Dickens, and the Misses Brontë, and Trollope and Thackeray! Nanny read them all to me, and I fear I still hear them in her voice. Tell me, do you think the Brontë sisters sounded 'Northern'? Mrs Vaux didn't, she just 'put it upon' for *Wuthering Heights*. 'T' maister nobbut just buried, and Sabbath not o'ered, und t' sound o' t' gospel still i' yer lugs, and ye darr be laiking!' Is *that* right? How wonderful to me it sounded. An incantation. And Shakespeare will make us happy forever. All of them being so much better than these outlandish caitiffs, the moderns, don't you agree? – However, *caitiff* is not idiosyncratic English, or is it? Do we *caitiff* nowadays? Yes? But you do not say *Yes*, you say *Oh yes* and smile, which means *No*. Dear me. How I wish I had more English friends who were alive, who could answer me back.

Sir, I know perfectly how the English shrink from acquaintance, especially abroad. But you are dining alone in this *trattoria*, unmentioned, surely, in any English guidebook, tucked away in a dingy piazza behind the opera, in unfashionable Cannaregio. You can only have elected to overlook its *décor* (these knick-knacks! Where can Apulio get them?) for the sake of its pure Venetian cuisine. And you are, if I may say so, sighing over your book –. I see. Baudelaire. How *worthy*. What a thing to face alone over dinner on a winter evening, even for a cosmopolitan Englishman. *Baudelaire!*

(Listen to that rain on the windows! 'The air so black,' so Nanny used to say, 'the water blacker still.' There will surely be *aqua alto* tomorrow.)

Therefore I wonder if you might, against the national character, accept interruption by a Venetian. Do not disquiet yourself: I am not a chatterer. If I have sensationalities in view, still I am as utterly discreet as yourself. I do not 'dine on' things – ('dine *out* on'? How odd. Thank you once more). I am an abyss. Rumours tumble into me, they are lost. Please go on with your *aperitif* untroubled. I am not pressing acquaintance. On the contrary. I impose myself not because you might divulge, but because, with such a face – if I may make so bold, sir – you must be apt to *retain*.

In short, I have something to tell you.

Moreover, I could not help over-hearing you order your dinner just now – not in good Italian as one might hope nay expect from such a one, but in something that was nigh to good *venexiàn*! Even Nanny, a deft linguist, never managed *that* in the end. You know that your Queen Elizabeth Tudor had one tutor to teach her French, another Spanish, another Latin, another Italian, and *another Venetian*? Yes of course you know that, of course. A man who knows to speak *venexiàn* and not *toscana* in such a *venexiàn* establishment, a man who knows to order *prosecco di Conegliano* with such familiarity: that is a man of the world, I say to myself, that man is deep in the water. Lagoon-water. Well .... *łe àneme generóxe łe vien oféxe pi da łe łuxinghe che dai insulti*. Generous souls are more offended by flattery than insult.

I cannot let this opportunity go past. I have something I think I need to unburden. No Venetian is fool enough to trust another Venetian with any serious secret. But you! A man evidently so sympathetic to the closed, fatal, wistful civilisation of this city, this republic! Surely, I tell myself, that is the man who might understand, who will not be appalled – who might even be amused.

Nonetheless.... *Chi che no domanda gnente el speta de tuto*, we say here. My final proverb, I promise. He who asks for nothing expects everything.

I wouldn't be presuming to intrude myself on you, despite all your worldliness, if it weren't for your otherworldly authority. Your holy orders, that is. Oh yes, Nanny did not so prevail with me as to *that* – indeed, her own prejudice really went not further than snubbing, mildly snubbing, the Anglican Chaplain here in Venice. She would not have denied; nor do I.

Sir: having told you what I have to tell you .... Our own priests – well, they keep secrets as well as a Venetian can, but what is that? And they are narrow, narrow. Beside, who knows? This is, perhaps, the first confession in history that is also a recipe. As a scholar, you might relish something so out of the way ....

All these ellipses. How shifty I must sound.

I say *confession*, and I recall the usual rules. 'It is under the seal, Master Paul,' Nanny used to say when refusing to tell me family secrets, although to be fair she generally betrayed them to me in the end. Peace be on her dust. She died here, as I think she wanted, and lies in San Michele.

But please! I do not mean anything sombre. Go on dining, listen with half of an ear. Drink your vermouth in peace, finish your nuts. I have nothing grim in mind. I have no objection to your writing it down. In your hotel room this very evening, for freshness of flavour. Even showing it to friends in a few years, no months, when I am beyond mortal reach – if you think anyone might be amused. But first, your hieratic act .... Where are you staying, by the way? Ca' Amadi? Ca' Amadi! Fie, sir, you keep astonishing me! That wonderful, unknown, lovely, hidden place! Where Frederick III came to sport with the Empress Leonora! Where Marco Polo dined!

My name is Trivisan, not an obscure name in Venetian history. Paolo Trivisan, Marchese di Foscari. I live, as of course you will deduce, in Ca' Trivisan. An interior unfinished and amazingly decrepit. But a splendid *façade* on a graceful curve of the Grand Canal, the *Canałasso* as we say, opposite Othello's palace, as you would call it. You've seen my house from a *vaporetto* chugging its way past all those the *palazzi*? Of course. You will remember they struck Proust as 'objects of nature, but of a nature which seemed to have created its works with a human imagination.' Is that how they strike *you*, signor? I was born in that sequence of *palazzi* and intend, this winter, to die in it. It's impossible for me to say what this place, this life, is like.

I am an elderly aristocrat, almost a dandy. Terrible paradox! The young can look distinguished by being merrily unkempt, but the old turn elegance itself into a sort of shabbiness. Behold this wrinkled skin, wrinkled like delicate silk we might say, wrinkled nonetheless. See how the fine cut of my cuff, a London shirter naturally, sets off knotted veins. Even your Englishness, your relative innocence, sets off *my* –.

Your name, might I – ? Felix! The fortunate one. Felice, as we degenerate Southerners say. Behold, Padre Felice, your antipasto has already arrived. *Sarde in saor* I delight to see. Eat, eat! Let my crimes be to you no more than the raisins and pine-nuts flecking these splendid marinated sardines.

I waste no more time on prologue.

The Venetian tourist office does not like to stress the fact, but you may nonetheless know that we have a serial killer, a sluggish yet persistent one, loose on our canals.

Of course these slayings, spaced-out over the last decade, have been interspersed with many a simple Venetian domestic murder, many a gangster assassination: crimes which, God knows, can have nothing to do with him. Yet it seems he exists, for his victims are suspiciously alike. Fat tourists from America, the Middle West, the New Jersey suburbs. They vanish, usually in couples. Casual witnesses sometimes describe them in conversation on their last evening with a Venetian well-spoken old gentleman – with me, in short. Or so the police allege. They claim that it is I who invite these travellers back to his *palazzo*. 'Awmagaw Elmer a real palace,' say the victims, apparently, 'we gotta see this.' And are never seen again.

Toward sunrise, more or less, the alarm is given at their uninteresting hotel. Then our *polizia* act out the same futile routine. They surround my *palazzo* on the land-side, and blockade its *façade* in silent lightless motorboats. Some drowsy magistrate makes out a warrant. Then they wait.

At dawn every day of the year, a fine old gondola lined with black velvet pulls out from the gloom of Ca' Trivisan, from the *palazzo* jetty, poled along by a saturnine gondolier in livery. Buried in a fur rug puffing a cigar in winter is – your servant. In summer I sketch patterns in the air with my black Turkish cigarette in its tortoise-shell holder, and I wear frankly incomparable whites, I wish you could see them, raw white silk from a place I know in the Æolian Islands. (Stromboli! The eternal smoke of the volcano! The infernal cavity on Vulcano! The colour of the sea at dusk!) I am at peace with the world. I am on my way to early Mass at Saluté.

But on gala mornings, mornings when there has been a killing the night before, I do not arrive at Saluté, for police-boats close in on me. Another vanished *straniero*? 'Alas,' I say, touching my breast lightly to prove my sincerity, 'alas;' but manifestly no *straniero* is on board my gondola.

Meanwhile their colleagues are ransacking my *palazzo*. They have gone over it again, again, so many times, finding nothing at all, despite their fatuous X-rays, their sonar, their electronic gadgets from Bangalore and Taiwan. There are no lardy American cadavers, absolutely nothing that would serve to dispose of one: no hiding places in the walls, no hidden doors.

The thing is impossible. I look, or so the policemen think, as guilty as I can be. But how on earth *could* an old man kill so many tourists and dispose of so many tourist corpses so quickly? Impossible. They let me go until next time. I resume my outdated life in my half-built, half-ruined, more-than-half-empty *palazzo*.

Really, most of it's literally empty. Our family n decline has chosen to shrivel rather than to fade. Our paintings and bronzes are largely evanishèd. All but half-a-score of rooms are shut up and putrefy unseen.

Still, the surviving rooms are almost as glorious as they have ever been, and the whole affair seems to impress my American visitors when I have them back. I bring them down little alleys where no one observes us except cynical Venetian cats, I let us in through a servants' door which looks like an indentation in the dank old brown battered brick. In we go, and they exclaim 'Oh my God' at tarnished gilt and battered stairs.

Americans can't walk, as everyone knows. They have such feeble bladders. They are exhausted by the stroll from wherever I found them, and the next thing out of their mouths is something like 'Where's the little boys' room?' That's the end of them.

There is one impressive-looking set of doors leading from the red drawing-room to the most important of bathrooms. 'Through those doors', I say, pointing, 'and then through a little door on your right. You'll have to step in and reach up for the light-pull.' 'How Old World,' they murmur if they're comparatively sophisticated, and that's the last I see of them.

The bathroom in question, you see, is important because it does not exist. I've said my place is half-built. One of my foremothers had a taste for internal plumbing, but to wall off a room is not to plumb it, and this bathroom was never put in. There was a non-existent floor marked by horizontal beams, overhanging a shaft. The shaft descends to water, to a long-since-flooded basement in fact, which communicates through a locked grille with the watery space where the gondolas live. In our childhood Ernesto and Patrizia-Anna and I would go down there. We would vanish. Nanny never understood where we went, or pretended not to. We would be all alone, scaring ourselves by clambering along those beams, dropping stones into the swaying black water below.

But those beams have mouldered away. Now it's a clean plunge.

(Clean, clear? – *Either?* Clean, then!) A *clean* plunge down to the water three floors down when you open the door. Which of course is usually bolted. Which I unbolt for these special guests.

If it's a couple on which I am lavishing the gift of eternal Venetian domicile, my technique is much the same. I show *numero uno*, usually the wife, into eternity, go back and chat for a few seconds to *numero duo*, and after a minute hint that he too has natural urges. 'There's another bathroom this way', I lie, and conduct him to the self-same fatal door.

One of them remarked passing through it 'I've never' (giggle) 'taken a dump in a palace before, 'cept in Las Vegas of course.' Rather nice last words, Felice? I mean, after a lifetime of, I presume, blather. 'Except in Las Vegas, of course', he smirked, stepping through – then the usual vanishing gasp or shriek – the usual profound splash – an instant or two of vague watery sound – stillness.

Only once did my *palazzo* let me down, which was unpleasant of it. I had just shown a black American, with buttocks of quite incredible bulk, like twin sacks of coal, into the lavatory, when I heard a most grating noise: a prolonged shriek, not the usual brief one. Then another. Then another.

I opened with ginger the door on nothingness –gingerly, gingerly – and saw ... nothing, of course. The next shriek, right at my feet, made me leap back with an oath, of which I repent. I beheld eight chubby dark fingers that ought not to have been there gripping. Somehow he had snatched as he plunged. *Cola spuza soto el naso*, which is our pungent Venetian way of saying *Yuk*.

It was an ethical dilemma. Should I simply go to bed and let gravity, acting on six decades of hamburger (O those ponderous buttocks wobbling in darkness, in mid-air!) do its healing work? But would I be able to sleep knowing a fellow creature was in mortal peril in my own house? Would that be chivalrous, would that be hostly? In any event, what if he managed the unimaginable feat of climbing back? Then he might find a door, a policemen, a horde of policemen, and plunge my life into great squalor.

'No, no', I told myself, 'courage, Trivisan! Think on your ancestors who fell in battle with the Turk! Act!' So, most unhappy, I went back into the red drawing-room and selected a smallish bust of ... Garibaldi! Which, now I think of it, is strange. Like everything else in changeless Ca' Trivisan, the bust became invisible to the family long ago, before I was born. But how can it have got there in the first place? My family always loathed Garibaldi and his ilk. (Is 'ilk' still a word?) Manin got one of us killed during the siege of 1848. A noisy fellow, Garibaldi! Perhaps he was a gift from Nanny. She felt a froward admiration for the goodly trouble-maker, I recall, as the English always do. Not you, though, perhaps?

Well, I bore this incongruous bust through to the abyss, and tapped it, much too gently to leave marks on the American gentleman's fingers, nor crass bloodstains on General Garibaldi. In the middle of a revolting howled obscenity, I regret to say, the fingers loosened and down he went. Plash. Struggle. Serenity.

It was a minute or two before I could bring myself to go back to the drawing room and replace the Founder of Modern Italy, so strong was my temptation to send him plunging into the darkness after Leroy. *Leroy,* there: I've remembered his name. But since the police were sure to raid my place on the morrow (and they did, they did), they might notice Garibaldi's absence and vex me with silly questions. My *palazzo* is so gloriously changeless, day by day, year by year, raid by raid. A little more decrepit as our civilisation fades, perhaps. A little dustier, to be sure, as Margharita, chief of my chambermaids, grows stiffer, more short-sighted. Well, let it be changeless yet. I replaced Garibaldi, patted him on his curly coif, and went sighing to bed.

That, revered Felice, was my only failure or near-failure. Except with Leroy, I hear almost nothing. I show them the doors, they pass through, a gentle splash, I finish my drink, I go to bed.

I have always been an early riser. Nanny's doing once more. Late to bed but early up. *Not* like Proust. *Not* like most Venetians. Do you know that at dawn the Canalasso is so still sea-birds roost on it? Like halcyons in the Greek fables. Never is Venice so nautical as before her first boat stirs, before her waters stir and shake, when her slug-a-bed inhabitants yet leave her alone. Then she is indeed a ship on the gull-jaunted open sea, but inverted, you understand, the sea gently running inside the ship, her cabins without. But still a ship, riding what is recognisably true sea, father Oceanus, largest of all tangible things in this world!

Felice, a thousand pardons. I have been carried off by love of my country. Venezia, that is, not Garibaldi's grotesque conglomeration 'Italia.' I was describing my trip down the Grand Canal to church.

Every morning I rise when it is dark, indeed *bruto* in December and January. I stand in the bay window of my *salone*, a brave prow as it feels, gazing up, gazing down. The light thickens and the first craft, bearing vegetables and fruits to market, cut the perfect virgin silk of the water. I stand there until it is time to go down to the gondolas and set out for church.

Such is my normal practice.

But on these gala mornings there is a difference. I strip off my clothes and go down to the flooded basements of my *palazzo*, the dusty lightless cellars.

I take with me from the pantry a box of pasta. *Strozzapreti*, buoyantly-named *priest-strangler*. You, Padre, *Felice mio*, a Venetian by grace if not by birth, will of course not misunderstand. In England it would be unthinkable. Can you imagine the shire folk naming some hairy half-digestible woodland berry (let us say) *parsonchoker*? That is not the English way. But just as sensitive husbands necessarily muse on poisoning their wives, so warm-blooded Catholic nations fantasise about gathering every cleric and religious and pope to our breasts to crush, to exterminate. This is how our imagination expresses its fervour, its fervour of affection. Even sophisticated Nanny, whose family had suffered so much for the Faith, could not grasp that. She was uneasy at the name.

As you know, priest-strangler is normally a short pasta, not what you'd expect from the name at all. However, my family, like certain other old Venetian families, has a tradition of getting our pasta especially made for us. We have ancient specifications of our own. The *strozzapreti* of the Trivisans is concocted for us by a pasta-maker by the Campo della Pescheria, who dyes it funereal black with *nero di Seppia*, and knows better than to sell it to anyone else. Perfect!

Ach, it's cold work in winter. In fact, almost penitential. Purgatorial. The bodies of my guests are not glorified by their night in that little square of cold brine. They are bloated. Those mysterious wallets they wear around their waists swell up like bladders. And as for their nylon clothing! *La bełésa ła xe 'nte l'ocio de chi che varda*, Beauty is in the eye of the beholder.

There's a heap of encaustic tiles from Verona down in the basement. My father planned a great staircase; it, like most of my father's projects, came to nothing. I slip a few of these tiles into the elasticated running-suits my people wear. I tow them through the water, opening the grille. I attach them to the keel of a gondola with the pasta, strand after strand of it. This is exhausting.

I climb up the stairs, I bathe and dress. By now the sun is coming up, even in winter. At quarter to eight I walk calmly down the main staircase. My gondolier hands me into the craft. Off we go to Mass.

On gala mornings, when I have a secret passenger, I appear as placid as always. But how my imagination riots! How it churns away beneath my gondola! I feel myself one with my poor bloated guest. Because I rest my hands on the gunwale (is that right? *gun'l*?) I can tell when dissolution has gone far enough. Tension on the strands of *strozzapreti* gently ceases, delicately, serenely. Then how lightly the gondola shoots forward, liberated.

It's Guiseppe on Mondays, Tuesdays, Thursdays and of course Sundays. Ahmed acts as my gondolier on Wednesdays, Fridays, Saturdays, and mornings after nights when Guiseppe made it into some foreign woman's hotel-room. They're fine fellows, both of them,. They feign not to know aught of unseen bodies, although they must notice the gracious moment when our gondola suddenly lightens.

If it is fine to feel that release, how beautiful it would be to watch the body slip silently away, through the green water into the deep ooze. Of course my whole purpose is to ensure no one sees it disposied of. But how I wish I could exempt myself!

Che fé Nettuno ammirar l'ombra d'Argo. Do you remember Dante's lovely line? Neptune boggles at the black bulk of Jason's ship, sweeping like a negative comet through the blue-green roof of his domain. The very last word in memorable surprise. Neptune, do I say? Rough old Neptune cannot be *duce* of the sea hereabouts. Not when our waters are so feminine, so yielding, so lustrous. Didn't our Doges wed the sea with a ring each year, in the days of Venetian freedom? Not Neptune, then, but one of his she-seneschals: a divine sea-naiad, a tritonette perhaps, some blonde, pink-white goddess wearing only pearls. She is our marine god. She it is who watches with astonished joy as my guests dance down through her waters.

Dawn light is beginning, turning her realm from black-green to lime. And into it breaks the improbably huge bulk of my tourist. He frees himself from my gondola to comes tumbling, diving toward her, twinkling his fingers, a solitary acrobat graceful as you may be sure he never was in life. Or if it be a couple, they dance a lazy *pas de deux* down into the murk, into the murk.

It's five metres, twenty feet as you might say, to the bed of the

Canalasso. Not that there is a clean bottom, just a haze of slime, mousse-like at top, then denser, blacker, until at last we reach impentrable mud, the true floor of the lagoon.

Of course it's dredged every so often. But why should I worry? Let us say one of my guests is scooped up; or even disdains to wait for the next dredging, and sheds his tile, bobbing to the surface. What then? He drowned, after all: authentically, uncomplicatedly drowned. The American Consulate despatches his half-dissolved corpse. The local newspapers in Nebraska or Nevada harrow their readers with the horrors of unlit alley-ways in 'Venice, Italy,' all leading down to deadly water. Fewer tourists come. *Eccellente.*

Anyway, it seems my all guests lie quiet in the Grand Canal. None have yet escaped the ooze. All thirty of them. Or forty? Not quite forty I think. I cannot be certain because I feel it vulgar to keep a tally, as if I were a lewd youth knotching fornications upon his bedpost. They're all there, rotting in rich comfortable silt.

Or not rotting. Obesity, cold, damp are the conditions for flesh to turn to *adipocere,* mortuary wax. You know this possibility? ... Thank you, learnèd father. I shall try to remember the scientific word for it. *Saponification.* Soapymorphosis in fact. Enemies, of which I have one or two, might insinuate something of the sort of me. Perhaps I have aged to what is hard and unfleshy. Decayed by Venice's chill waterways as I am.

Basta! As a clergymen you must be used to the freshly dead. Yet you are not finishing your sardines. You frown? Am I correct in calling that subtle expression a frown? Why? No, no, eat – do not speak. Let me speculate. It cannot be physical disgust, that is beneath you. Can it be moral unease? Might you (it seems incredible; but the English conscience is so opaque), might you be thinking that my victims didn't want to die? That I might almost be said to have murdered them against their will?

Impossible thought! *Will,* my honoured Felix, *will* means nothing except in a properly formed male adult. Indeed, it means nothing except in a man bred with the extraordinary liberty and discipline of the *nobilità,* in which category I number, preëminently in fact, the English gentleman.

I am not, Father Felice, some sort of residual Nieztschean fascist. Do not grimace. I am humane enough. But hear me. My so-called victims are scarcely weaned, one sees as much by what they ask for in restaurants. They are, in their own outlandish dialect, *anally-fixated*. Abortive babies, that is, mewling to be done away with. Or if you like, roses, inciting one to pluck. A rose is bred for nothing but to cry to the man strolling past 'Observe my dewy petals, my gorgeous hue. Snip me, sir, house me in a procelain bowl.' Can it be said to will its continued life? Perverse!

Besides…. Let me speak with almost lunatic boldness, excusing a moribund man his frantic delusions, perhaps slanders….

I am sceptical of your moral scepticism, *Felice mio*. You scowl; yet somehow it is a scowl I cannot credit. There is in your face a mark which I recognise. No, I cannot think I am mistaken. You too are a man who has washed off virginity, virginity I mean not of *eros* but of *thanatos*. You've killed, that is to say. You too know what it is to cleanse the world of the only filth that truly defiles. You have shed blood, which is the one means of cleansing.

Yes, yes, I detect it in your demeanour, priest though you be! I acknowledge a fellow vengeful angel. How strange that I should meet you by chance, as if by chance…. But hush, Trivisan, hush. You sin against the laws of hospitality. And Felix, forgive me. What was meant to be merely *my* confession *to you* seems to have stirred an echo, a backwash, an (admiring) denunciation *of you*. That was not my intention.

Listen. Your fish are gone, and I want to tell you an aspect of my crime which even you will not have experienced yourself. There is a dark side to my little hobby, a hint of violation. Of cannibalism.

After my first killing, which was very much an *impromptu* let me stress, I came home from Mass meditating on the removal the evidence, of which there wasn't much even that first time. My guest had already bedded down in the *Canalasso*. He had already set out on his transmogrification into loose bones, or – how much more wonderfully! – into a ghostly soap statue of himself.

I polished the doorknobs to remove fingerprints. I re-bolted the deadly doors. What of the pasta, though, the twenty or thirty broken strands still dangling down the flanks of my gondola? I removed them with a butter-knife. But why throw them away, why? My *strozzapreti* had become, under the prodigious weight of my Americans, extraordinarily stretched; softened, too, by immersion in the brine of the canals; subtly flavoured with Venice herself. These long precious strands were too soft to boil. I simply turned them over raw in butter, with pepper and slices of white truffle. I had stumbled over – I beg your pardon? 'Stumbled upon', aha! Thank you! I had stumbled *upon* a classic. Something quite astounding.

Allora! Your *risotto al Nero di Seppia* has arrived. Time for a digression. We ought to divert ourselves from death and cadavers. Let me see ....

Is this the moment? Perhaps it is well past the proper moment. The moment, I mean, to mention that my mother, for so many decades the Marchesa di Foscari, was by birth a Miss Milly Levy Newsome of Wollett, Mass. A Jewess on her own mother's side and a considerable heiress in ... well, a kitchen implement. Not a peeler, not a scrubbing-brush, nothing quite so bad. I am confessing my own mortal sins, not prenatal blemishes. An implement, let us say. Nanny would sometimes laugh over it. The only unkindness with which I entax her. Mama's father made this implement by the million, died and left her a mountain of dollars. She hurried her mountain to Europe, lightly chaperoned, married my father and went native. Refused to speak that outlandish *(bizzarra)* language, English. Became Catholic as Catholic can be. Liked to put it about that her maiden name was *Signorina Melisenda dei patrizi de Woollett*: Miss Milly of the Woollett nobs. Is that not a charming fantasy?

Well, Mama introduced me, in her bad Italian, to the following problem.

Her former God, the Jewish one, is tremendously keen on forbidding His chosen people things which, after all, He made, and made most attractively. *Ciò che un sacco di cose che Dio ha fatto per noi di non mangiare.* That's how she used to sneer at her former co-religionists. Her Italian was never very good, and as for her Venetian, well; *Signorina* Elizabeth Tudor would have winced.

But there is one creature Jehovah positively presses on His chosen people, a chosen sea-creature called the *hillazon*. If you kill a *hillazon* and treat it in the right way you get dye of a particular shade, extremely dark blue. Jehovah insists on this. It's His favourite colour, evidently. He prescribes it dozens of times, for the High Priest's vestments, the tapestries in the Temple, and the tassels to be affixed to the corners of clothes. Jewish tradition says the dye must come from *hillazon*. There are dreadful penalties specified if you cheat and use the indigo plant instead. That's quite the wrong shade.

Why is God so keen on almost-black purple-blue? Mama raised the question. My answer, which I yield to the tribunal of mother Church, and in the meantime to you my dear *padre*, is that Almighty

God finds He has slightly overdone the solar radiance of paradise. *Urbs Sion aurea: Jerusalem the golden, with milk and honey blessed* – milk and honey, sun glittering on bullion: a yellow-white, silver-gold palette. Like the papal flag. Splendid but wearing. God has, or might expect His courtiers to have, a certain nostalgia for the more umbrous, nocturnal tints of earth. Dark-purply-blue is as far from the tonic values of gold as we can get…. Does this convince you? Oh well. Perhaps one day Rome will uphold my doctrine.

There's no call for High Priest's vestments since Titus burned the Temple. Yet pious Jews would still like to dye their tassels blue, if only they could be sure it was the right blue, the right creature. Most of them cautiously leave their tassles white.

For what *was* the *hillazon*, exactly? One theory is: a sort of sea-snail. *Pfui!* A much happier rabbinical thought is that *hillazon* is *sepia officinalis*, the common cuttlefish, which dyes pasta black as you see before you this instant, but wool (note this) dark-blue. Cuttlefish! A delectable idea. I applaud the rabbis who propound it. I applaud the unsceptical Jews who sport dark-blue tassels. I applaud the capitalists who profit from the renewed demand for cuttlefish ink.

Even for us Catholics, much turns on this question: is *hillazon* the same as *sepia officinalis*? Or rather is *sepia officinalis* the same as *hillazon*? For if it is, God's preference for dark-blue-purple means there must be cuttlefish in heaven. There must, there must. God has lavished unusual amounts of imagination on cuttlefish, more, one might almost say, than on that clumsy simian man. Cuttlefish have three hearts, you know, and green-blue blood; they can change colour more swiftly and precisely than chameleons – they're a sort of cinema screen, in fact – and they're the most intelligent of all invertebrates. (I'm not quite sure how this is measured; it's what I've read.) They're buoyed effortlessly by their cuttlebone, unique to them, which jewellers prize. Their eyes are the best in nature, however *that* is measured, and have pupils shaped, say the dull scientists, like a smooth letter W – or rather, I say, like omega, ω, culminating letter of the Greek alphabet. A hint I propose that when history is consummated in glory, when God has become the Alpha and the Omega, as He says He must, cuttlefish will be there, after the end of all else. Are not you and I, honoured sir, with our flickering colour and uncommon blood, cuttlefish in our souls?

And might not God be a cuttlefish?

I propound no heresy. We not they are made in His image. But isn't possible that along some infinite dimensions, from certain seraphic perspectives, God might also appear to have cuttlefishish qualities? Oh, that crushingly thin English smile of yours! Very well, I withdraw my more extreme doctrine. I recant, I recant.

But the ink, the ink! *That* I maintain, for *that* I would go to the stake. Amidst the orange nectar, the gilt-yellow ambrosia, the cream and honey tones of the everlasting City, there are without doubt ponds of cuttlefish to supply us everlastingly with dye for our robes. And surely, surely, also for the table. The ceaseless wedding feast of the Lamb cannot be all ambrosia and nectar, those white-gold dishes. God must sometimes add a darker grace-note.

Think of it! Cherubim blast a fanfare from trumpets of silver. There is applause, wild cries of *Hosanna*, a modulation even in the redoubled rapture of the blessed. Amethyst doors swing open on the banqueters, revealing glimpses of radiant cloudscape over the shoulders of servant-angels, who are bearing in: a course of *risotto al nero di seppia*. This, then, is the most eternal of mortal dishes. *Quod erat demonstrandum*.

But, eternal though it be, you have finished it. Apulio! – It comes. *Fegato di mongana alla veneziana*. How well, if I may say so, *padre* Felix, honoured sir, you have chosen. You know this recipe comes from the *L'Apicio moderno*, which Francesco Leonardi published in the last years of our Republic? Already the old order was breaking up when Leonardi wrote, already that monster Buonaparte was on his career of desolation. (Tuscan by origin, the Buonapartes, like so many terrible things.) But Leonardi was recording our divine simplicity, our way with the liver of a milk-calf, for instance. This same *vitella da latte*. Just onions, oil, white wine, butter, a little broth, pepper, salt. As it's served, lemon juice and a touch of parsley. Behold. Perfect, perfect.

Flesh-eating is the climax of dinner. Absolution is the climax of confession. The moment has come. For these and all the sins of my life, and any that I cannot now remember, Father, I ask penance and absolution from – no, no, dear man, don't make any flamboyant cruciform gestures in the air! This *trattoria* is owned by a good Communist, very squeamish, easily upset. Your fork will do: just sketch, if you would, the divine gallows on a small scale, silently, while I bow my unworthy head over this unfortunate checked cloth. I am imagining your voice pronouncing in my head *Ego te absolvo ab omnibus censuris et peccatis in nomine Patris....*

Yes, yes. *Grazie mille, un milione di loro.*

I am at peace, most curiously at peace.

And yet, even more curiously, I am not. 'Curiouser and curiouser!' says Alice in her book, which Nanny seemed not to find disturbing at all. Please do not let your veal spoil. Savour it, let me rabbit. No, rabbit *on*, of course. A strange idiom…. Why, I ponder to myself, why are you so curiously unlike any conceivable cleric, not matter how schismatical? Hm? Why was that stroke-stroke with your fork so very embarrassed, and as it happens back-to-front?

Is it possible, Father, or rather *not* father, *brother. Hypocrite auditeur, – mon semblable, – mon frère!* Even Nanny, you understand, excellent woman, did not read me Baudelaire; that came at a later date…. Is it possible you are not what you seem? Or rather, exactly what you *seem*, that is, an artist of killing, but not what you *dress*? That you are a laic in disguise, and presumably here in Venice 'on a job' if that is really proper American slang?

I see it is so. Pray do not pause over your *vitella*. I would not think of asking to what you are up. Felix is really your name, though? … I see, and *Culpepper* to rhyme with *vulpa*, Romansch for *fox*. Very well. God indeed adds a darker grace-note. We are in fresh territory.

In that case, since I am after all unshriven, let me confess something else. No don't twitch, gentle sir; it's not another sin to the account of Paolo Trivisan. Were I truly absolved, for the moment perfectly sinless, sitting before you pure as a baby, I might still tell you *this*. The homicide to which I refer was set in motion by quite another *grand seigneur*. To use a language for which I do not greatly care. I have, forsooth, an ancestral feud. Chad, father to dear Mama of whom we have spoken quite enough, frittered away his twenties in Paris with *une femme d'un certain âge*. He left her with a pang, chivvied by his New England kindred. And to revenge himself on his family, or his cast-off mistress, or both, my grandfather married presently a Manhatten girl with lots of raw new money. He never visited France again, perhaps dared not, and passed on a prejudice which after all is a little beneath me. What was I saying, though? That I have heart disease. There have been incidents. Once last year was carried off prone in one of those waterborne ambulances foreigners admire so much. I lay drugged, watching the cornices of the palaces swim together and apart, together and apart, like lines of dancers at balls.

The doctors use big words and comfortable turns of grammar, future conditionals which I am in no condition for. I near my end. My series of – very well, let us call them what yellow journalism would call them – my murders, my tourist assassinations, my pasta massacres: that series has surely reached its last term already. Absolved or not, those sins lie behind me. A few more weeks, at most a few more months, and I die.

Now. Of course you have ordered no *dolce*. You are going to have cheese, doubtless one of the great cheeses of our region, asiago, montasio, acidino, taleggio from the Venetian *terra firma*. You are a Northern gentlemen with none of our childish tooth for sugars. But indulge me this once, this first and last supper of ours. Divine forgiveness, even if bogus, calls for something sweet. Have you ever had true Venetian *sgroppino*? No? Glorious! I feared you were too cosmopolitan to be surprised. *Apulio, il mio amico! Alcuni sgroppino per questa inglese ecclesiastico splendido, la prego! Pronto!* I think you will be surprised. – Look, here comes Apulio already with his trolley. See, two bowls. This one of lemon ice-cream, made this afternoon of heavy cream from cows grazing in the vale of Belluno. In this bowl, strawberries from some sunny island far down the Dalmatian coast, an island that was, and should be, and shall be once more, Venetian. Ripe, cold, puréed *fragoli*. And this is of course *prosecco*, the dry sparkling glory of Valdobbiadene in alpine Veneto, just below the snows. See how Apulio beats the three together. And into – ah: *la poexìa ła xe l'arte de far entrar el mar int'un bicer*, poetry is the art of putting the ocean into a glass. A Venetian saying.

Would it be fanciful, do you think, to call *sproggino* the essence of Venetian civilisation? So yielding, sweet, elusive, so enveloping, like the all-receiving mud of the canals? Since Buonaparte and the Hapsburgs filched our empire, what is there for us to do but relish our own effeminate sweetness? We are far gone in decadence. Who knows: possibly my little crimes (*not* blotted out in the sight of God, after all) are the final glimmer of the martial glory of Venice.

Have you heard of Ruzante? One of our 'dialectal' poets, as our insolent Tuscan tyrants-of-language would have it. You have? Ah, then, you are in truth a Venetian by adoption! This is what Ruzante wrote five centuries ago, when after all we were still a martial republic of sorts: *E che a foesse stò amazò in campo*. What if I had been slain on the battlefield, if war had made of me a ghost? *E che a foesse el me spirito?* That would be lovely, *Lo sarae ben bela*. But no damn it, ghosts can't eat! As a boy, I never heard that line without thinking of *sproggino*. *No, càncaro, spiriti no –*.

'Gawd Wilmer, it's a slushy. Oh my Gawd, will you just look at that over there.'

– *spiriti – spiriti no – mango.*

'Where, Laverne, where?'

'There, you klutz, over *there*. That young guy, the clergy, with the old guy. At that table in the corner. Get an eyeful of what he's chowing on. It's a *slushy*.'

'Why, so it is. Looks awful like a regular slushy, anyhow.'

'Who'd've thought?'

'Yeah, who'd've thought? – Say, do you reckon they'd mind if I took a snap, Laverne?'

'Wilmer! Put that away! D'rectly, y'hear! Remember what that man said in the hotel in London, England? In Europe there are places where a body just don't take pictures! They're powerful refined over here. I'm surprised at you. I guess we shouldn't even be staring at them like this, as if we was no-count trash. Look, the young guy's stopped munching and he's kinda looking back at us. Sorta weird.'

'Awh, that don't matter none. No way can they speak English, anyways not good enough to understand *us*. They wouldn't be attending to us, nohow; this is jist our everyday inside voice.'

'No, honey, over here they whisper to each other inside. I've seen 'em at it. You can't make out one word just from a few tables away, even if they're British folk speaking regular English.'

'Anyways, Laverne, I sure want to know what you calls a slushy in *Eye*-tell-yun, that's all, so as I could have one too. In fact, lots of 'em. A supersized slushy with everything. Look at this on my plate now! I asked for a low-cal burger with double fries extra over easy – you heard me – and I'm getting powerful anxious about it.'

'Wilmur! Is *it* playing up again? You shoulda *said*, Huggy-Bun, you shoulda said.'

'It's purdee chronic down there, Squiddgy-Pie, it's purdee chronic. I ran out of Clear-Floe-Anal-yze cream in Paris, France, jist before we got on the plane. And you know it's the wrong voltage to work our ornery sphincter-massagers.'

'Well anyways that squishy's probably not all it's cracked up to be, either, The young guy's just done *spluttered* his up all over his *serviette*.'

Coraggio, caro Padre falso, coraggio. – Sir! Madam!

'(Wilmer!)'

Might I –

'(Laverne! The old Italian guy's speaking! To us!)'

– might I say how gratified I am, how grateful Venezia is, to have you within our borders.

'(.... Say something, Wilmer. Say something.)'

'Er. Gee whiz, sir, you speak English. Speakee the English!'

'(English! Lan'sake Wilmer, he sounds like he was British or something!)'

'Yeah. Er. Fact, you – speak – English – real – swell – considerin' that ....'

(*O mi sento il diavolo entro suscitare, il mio amico!*)

'In fact, it hardly sounds like you was foreign. Hardly at all.'

'Tell him we're from the You Ez of Ay.'

'(Shush, Laverne. I figure he knows.) Um: it sure is swell being in this town, sir. Though powerful hard to find your way around. We musta walked for five hours trying to find our hotel, and then Laverne saw this little place and said Wilmer, I just can't go another darn step, and in we came. We ain't used to walking about so. I should say, Laverne and me, we don't walk nowhere. We're pretty significant folk in Knob Lick.'

'(*He may not have heard of Knob Lick, Wilmer. Tell him.*)'

'Knob Lick, Missourah, sir.'

(My friend, my friend: can he really have said "Knob Lick"?) Honoured madam, honoured sir: I am Paoli Trivisan. A marchese as it happens. The rain, although dreadful, is lessening. My *palazzo* is not so far from here. I beseech you to come back with me once you have dined. I will give you brandy and send you home in my gondola. Home to your hotel is what I of course mean.

'Um. Um. – (*Laverne! – speak up, do.*)'

'Well – Wilmer and I don't mind if we do, Mista Trivisan. That's mighty neighbourly.'

When you are ready, then. Finish up, gentles! My young friend here is just going. (*Si, si, senor inglese, via, via.* Do not even think of paying, Felix, do not think of it. This is my dinner. The pleasure is mine, the profit is mine. Go back to Ca'Amadi and write our conversation up. But listen, seriously, in your ear. Thanks be to the sportive Fates I was not on "the receiving end" of an absolution which I would not dare waste, not with time so short. But you were wonderfully false. I am still free. I have not been lifted blameless to the threshold of paradise. I am still in the world. Or rather, I am still bathed in the wholesome flames of purgatory. Sin flourishes and is charred away, flourishes and is charred. There is no reason not to splatter my soul with a little more cuttlefish ink. One last splash of heavenly blackness. It seems ghosts do eat, now and then. For, Felice – *domine reverindissime* – *mio caro, bello* – I fear there are about be two more disappearances from Venice. Two more foreigners gone to the realm of bright light, mitigated, if my theory is correct, by hillazon. You understand me. The police will call at dawn as usual. I have no doubt they will soon let me go. And so I shall expect you for lunch. At one. You know what we will have. Time for renewed repentance afterward, time for remorse over the *dolce*, coffee, liqueurs. Purgatorial penitence. But for now farewell, good night –.) Well, my dear American guests?

'We're ready for it.– Night, young fella. Night. Night. Hope we ain't chasing your young friend away!'

Not at all, sir. See him scurry into his great-coat and hat. He has pressing business elsewhere. (Is it not so? Write, write.) Shall we go?

'Sure thing. I'll just settle up. Gar-kon!'

'(Wilmer! The folks at the Knob Lick Country Resort ain't never gonna believe we done have a drink with a real live Venice-ish lord.)'

'(They never will, Laverne. They never will.) Gar-kon! Gar-kon! The check!'

III.

Icknield

or,

The Castaway of Britain

A Christian *must* be attracted to fetid carcases, as hyenas are, or Baudelaire, or the angel of the Resurrection.

GIUSEPPE, PRINCIPE DE
LAMPEDUSA

CHAPTER 1
Difficulties of a silk

i.

No that's not it, Ralph Bolswood wasn't trying to make himself invisible. He was trying to travel forward in time to be invisible there. The invisibility he craved exists only in the future, in other people's coming states of brain. When the police posters appear, when his photograph begins popping up on television and in the *Daily Telegraph* paper and online editions (the day after tomorrow? the day after that?), he wants to be like air in the minds of the thousands of people now looking at him.

Or looking through him, since he was invisible, invisible. Inaudible as well he hoped, although however he tried, he couldn't stop himself murmuring 'Sorry, sorry' to the four o'clock rabble as he elbowed it aside. At least he was sure he was odourless. He had been careful not to touch his usual stuff that morning, on the fantastic grounds that someone might remember the passing splendour of cologne from Trumpers' of St James'.

So here he was, apologetically jostling his way through Marylebone Station, featureless, immaterial, without attributes, invisible, intangibly pushing past sweaty bodies. Bodies which had also, evidently, abstained from scenting themselves. He was pressed against dozens of them, yet he hoped to be like the girl he suddenly remembered from a childhood story – a Lappland princess, was it? – who had the knack of leaving no track when walking over fresh snow.

He'd bought this specially dull overcoat last week, for no other reason than it looked so average. 'It is precisely the sort of thing I never wear.' (Or *wore*. One of the suicide's unanticipated burdens is finding it awkward to keep using the present tense.) 'In the days when I put on clothes, I never put on things as dreary as this coat. And I normally wouldn't dream of owning a baseball cap.' (*Would not normally have dreamt.*)

The baseball cap was, Ralph thought, his masterstroke. On the one hand it hid his face from the security cameras that infest London; he only had to keep the flap low. But on the other hand, it was part of the recognised uniform of negation. Everywhere middle-aged men, even fellows in decent suits, wore them. 'I am nobody,' that is surely what they proclaim, 'ignore me, I'm so pusillanimous I stole this from my ten year-old's wardrobe.' Ralph cleared the ticket barrier. 'These men can't all', thought Ralph, stirred out of self-concern for an instant, 'be suicides trying to be invisible in the future, can they?' (*Can they have been?*)

But this was no moment for whimsy. He was approaching his train. Passengers always glare at new passengers as they board. Even with his inconspicuous black cap, High Street raincoat and studied shamble, this was where he risked leaving a trace. 'Oh yes, officer, I remember that face. A distinguished-looking gentleman who got on at Marylebone and stood at the back of the carriage. He got off at High Wycombe.' 'Aha, you old biddy, little did you realise that I got off, walked up the platform, and got on again. I didn't really leave the train until Saunderton.' He had thought of this. He had thought of everything. He had been disciplined, he'd taken no risks. Well, except for the 'phone call to his boy in the morning –

છ

08:06. *Bring bring. Bring bring. Bring bring. Beep.*

'Hi. You've reached Tristan Bolswood's voicemail. If you who know you are. And you know why you rang. You know what to do.' *Beep!*

'Um, Tristan. Sorry to miss you. This is daddy. Father. Ralph. Nothing much – apologies for ringing early, well earlyish, sorry about that. Just if you were in – but you're not. I was thinking of you, and I'll be thinking of you this evening, but don't bother ringing back, not then – sorry-sorry, not making much sense. So. I think that's it. That is it. Good-bye then'

છ

– that was all. He'd 'phoned because he'd suddenly needed to hear his son's voice one last time. Of course it hadn't worked. The boy hardly ever answered. But he'd just left a message, keeping it light, not a farewell, nothing to suggest intent. Tristan wouldn't think anything of it.

Nobody would think anything. He'd behaved so normally all day. One moment (he'd looked at his watch: eleven past three) Sir Ralph Bolswood, K.B.E., Q.C., *Ralph* to rhyme with *strafe* not *self*, was leaving his chambers in Middle Temple. 'Um, goodbye. Miss Flank.'

''Bye, Sir Ralph,' Angela had said in her untrustworthy voice. 'Ever such awful snow out there.'

'Yes, I'm so sorry, I should have said – and I'm told it's due to get worse in an hour. Do be – well. Careful home!'

The next moment he'd been snatched out of this world, never to be seen again. That is, he'd donned his appalling new raincoat in the lobby of his chambers where no one could see him, and (waiting until he was past the porters and in the street) got the unspeakable baseball cap out of his pocket and pulled down over his eyes. 'It was the moment I ceased to exist,' thought Ralph, gazing out the train window at the thickening blizzard. 'I put on garments of invisibility, I vanished from the sight of men. Now I'm just tidying away a corpse. I'm already in the void.'

Self-pity was getting the upper hand. He'd known uncharacteristic, frantic joy just outside the Temple, flinging his cellphone into a skip. It had been his ball and chain for many years. He'd tossed it so hard he'd heard it shatter. And then he'd felt quite gleeful riding a number 13 'bus to Marylebone. This was a calculated step, cab rides being easy to trace. What he hadn't anticipated was the thrill. It was, what, ten years since he'd been on a double-decker. It gave him the sense of a schoolboy stunt, much as it would have seemed, when he really was a schoolboy, exciting to take a taxi. As the train pulled out of Marylebone he'd had the sensation of becoming 'to all intents and purposes', as he liked saying in court (*cliché* slackens the mind of rival counsels, relaxes witnesses; Bolswood thrived on contempt), dead, permanently invisible. He'd evaporated; and this had given him a spasm of delirious escape.

But that had been in London. Now he was in God-knows-where, wildest Middlesex perhaps. Snow was making the world invisible, implausible, dubious. And almost impassible: anyway, the train kept slowing and stopping, slowing and stopping. Maybe God, repenting of Middlesex, was blotting it out. Bolswood, too, was asking himself – late in the day, but he had to think of something – whether these manouevres had a point. Was it really necessary not just to die but to dematerialise? Why hadn't he simply done the thing at home, leaving Łucja to discover him dangling from the banister? Or indeed the Guilty Party? (He'd recently started calling her this, not 'Serena', not 'my wife'. Breach of Contract, which was his specialty, ate deep into what did for his soul.) Yes, there'd have been a certain grim justice in having his body found by the Guilty Party.

But the Guilty Party was in Tuscany for who could say how long. Her international shopping expeditions were formless. Nor did Ralph like the idea of hovering for days in mid-air above the Burmese teak in the hall, perhaps dripping onto the chessboard marble squares. Also, the thought of Tristan had given him pause. Tristan did sometimes pop home from 'varsity unannounced. Ralph couldn't bear the thought of being found by his son, whom he loved with such anguish of apology it felt, really, much like love.

Then there was afterward. He'd been to suicides' funerals – had been to one only a few months before, a judge who'd gone under a train, horribly superior fellow, no reason given, a great surprise all round, perhaps an inspiration. Wasn't Mr Justice MacPharlain Ralph's model? Wasn't it then the seed had been planted that was so flowering so luxuriantly now, this snowy afternoon? Hadn't he been, even then, a little jealous?

But the funeral! All such funerals! Vicars nowadays seem incredulous of immortality, infernal or otherwise. Since they can't speak of the life to come, they have to drone on about life past: 'Happy, happy memories of our belovèd friend. Yes, he had his burdens. Burdens which drove him at the last to this unfortunate step. Yet so much, so very much of what we recall of him is joyous. Is it not?'

But at funerals the so-called mourners aren't recalling the cheery past, they're wondering about the present. They sit staring at the coffin, trying to imagine what's under the lid. Ligature marks round the neck, fist-sized opening in the skull, black face for the poisoned, general pulpiness for jumpers, bloating for drownees, flaking for the burned.

Not Bolswood. When hope of his return was gone they'd hold his memorial in the Temple Church, with an oblong of air where the coffin ought to be: a space of cleanliness, an intense gap in the brickwork of the universe. Everyone could stare at that.

Yes. Far better to do as he was doing. No body for nobody. *Fade far away, dissolve, and quite forget,* he told himself, *The weariness, the fever, and the fret.*

With such mental fidget he passed north and west, toward the spot he had chosen, keeping his mind from the positive misery of death-in-life.

ii.

Who is this wearing little man? Why are you being asked to find amusement in his suicide?

Ralph Ackerley Bolswood was born in 1958, was sent to Winchester where he did well although not at games and was unpopular, went as a scholar to Oxford, where he did well even at games and was unpopular, and so to the Bar and triumph after triumph – how, exactly?

There was nothing much to look at. His fingers were so long they could perform disturbing crablike motions up and down up his lapels. Otherwise his was a humdrum body: middling height; good but watery, blinking green eyes; flaxen hair thin but not inclined to recede. His clear skin was peppered with red moles or beauty spots which had to be checked every year to see if they would turn cancerous; they never did. He was broad cheek-boned and smooth browed, in that very English way which can look faintly Chinese. His chin was dimpled.

Not that you'd have noticed any of these features if you'd met him. His face simply bore the shape LAWYER. In all the professions, Nature is subdued to work. The professional becomes a superhuman *thing*; that's why the professional player of games or reader of books or maker of prayers strikes us as uncanny. In Bolswood's case, veracity, hesitation, openness, fair-dealing, shame and doubt had been gouged from the original face. He looked distinguished, but he also looked monstrous, like a quarried hill. At the age of fifty-five, he appeared not so much a man – a noun, a fathomless *being* – as an all-too-obvious verb. Here is lawyering. Makes Strong Lies.

How did he prevail over the other liars? It was his fidget of apology. Far more than most Englishmen, Ralph Bolswood was compelled to keep explaining to the universe that he had not chosen to exist, and would stop existing if only he could. He never attained the brazenness of accepting his own existence. He was never content to be one consciousness, which he could not escape, flowing along beside billions of consciousnesses, which he could not enter. Most men find this situation so obvious they never notice it. Bolswood could not endure it. He was a smudge on the glass of reality. Hose down the outside and it seemed to be on the inside; scrub the inside and it seemed without.

His horror at being went beyond (or fell below) self-dislike. He

envied the calm, unblinking and well-informed self-dislike of many
of his colleagues. He could never reach the detachment necessary for
liking or disliking or even pitying himself. It was his existence that
seemed unendurable, not his attributes.

I have forgotten to mention Bolswood's voice. This matters a great
deal at the Bar, where voices are more individual than faces. Perhaps
that's true of the human voice everywhere. Few people make a habit of
analysing sounds; most people make a mystery of why they're repulsed
or attracted. It's noise nice or nasty that sways you. It's not her 'aura'
that grates, but her harsh rhotic stops: she says *butter* with a great snarl
at the end, so of course she seems to you a hard woman.

In any case, at the Bar they do analyse; there's a connoisseurship
of voice. Bolswood's was held to be good, a resonant baritone, not
buoyant or energetic but effortlessly varied, with a noble violin lilt for
specious elation, a shady oboe rumble for affected grief, and excellent
clear timbre, as of a piano's white keys, when telling outright lies. Yet
none knew better how to sound parched and dreary when retailing the
argument of his opponent.

He possessed a beautiful, intricate, powerful weapon, which
had nothing to do with his nature, and which he wielded for squalid
purposes. Even so certain paranoid regimes in Asia luxuriate in their
atomic bombs.

Bolswood's table-talk would not look funereal written down, so
I'm not going to give you any of it. It was the air of wishing he did
not have to speak at all that was so harrowing. It was 'Sorry.' Anything
provoked apologetic words – or not even words. He had a particular
noise, which Tristan learned to recognise before he could speak, and
was soon able to imitate (and name 'the daddy-noise'): a sort of snorting
cough swallowed high in the palate. And there was 'Sorry-sorry' said
with extraordinary speed, the second 'Sorry' retracting the first.

'Sorry-sorry', and the daddy-noise, and Bolswood's apologetic
manner, were devastating in court. He was regarded with terror because
he knew how to make himself so dismal. The acid of radical self-
doubt was most effective sprayed over expert testimony. But ordinary
witnesses learned to dread Bolswood too. He could lead them along,
making them so sorry for him that they'd supply words, finish phrases,
colour in the gaps, and find themselves ruining their case. Even other
lawyers would bend to cater to Bolswood's craven embarrassment,
putting themselves off-balance, and ending up, they couldn't quite

understand how, on the losing side.

Bolswood was dogged as a dung-beetle, and fearfully clever and so forth. But there's not much in that. Everyone at the English Bar is fearfully clever, in about the same degree and in the same way, just as most barristers possess assiduity and interesting voices. Yet Bolswood was preëminent. And it was abnegation that did the trick.

Abnegation, whatever its professional use, is tricky as the raw material of a marriage.

Serena was not a demanding woman. She would have endured any amount of fretfulness, and any coldness toward herself, her emotional standards having been fixed by her own father. But Ralph's coldness toward himself baffled and finally repelled her.

She had married Ralph six weeks after meeting him at a house-party in Scotland because he was managing, handsome enough and well-bred, all things considered. Despite his undertaker manner, there was a certain charm, which she didn't try to pin down. It was, of course, simply his voice. He was spoken of as a rising figure at the Bar. He would do. After all, men were uniform as 'buses. They were hearty and selfish, like her brothers and father and grandfathers. She wished to be possessed, she wished to be carried along toward death; it was time; she boarded the next one that passed.

There's no point in being shocked by Serena. The 'Eighties produced her type in industrial quantities, as a by-product of brassy feminism. Careeristes despised mere wives as cravens. Mere wives and mere-wives-to-be, accepting this view of themselves, became more compliant than women had ever been before.

But even a trophy wife needs some force of ego to be pliant before, and Ralph didn't offer that. Slowly, slowly, as she bore and raised the only child she would permit, Serena grasped that his endless apologies weren't convention. They weren't pretence, they had nothing to do with courtesy. He wasn't shy and he wasn't humble. He simply had no loyalty to his own self. He regretted existing not because he was penitent about his character, but because the organ of self-love had shrivelled when he was, for all we know, still in the womb.

୦୪

9:50. *Ka-ring ka-ring. Ka-ring ka-ring. Ka-ring ka –*

'*Słucham?* Hallo?' A guttural voice. 'This is the house of Sir

Bolswood and his wife also and Mr Tristan the son of them also.'

'Good morning. Well, goodish. What a lot of snow. Is Sir Ralph there, please? His mobile seems to be dead.'

'No he is goned. This is Łucja only the housekeeper of him. You speak message, I write message thus, perhap he read message.'

'Would you tell him –'

'No I not tell him. He say thus: "You take day off Łucja, two day off, three, here money, you be gone do fun, I eat dinner at club only." Now thus I putting on my hat and boots also for snow which surely worse will be and then worse and to my sister in Slough I go.'

'But will he get a message this evening?'

'I know not that. I know not what he do. I know not if I see him more. "Thank you for all," he say, "Łucja." Never he speak to me thus. He is a man so English. So polite but oh so cold, always he say "Sorry" never he say "Thank you". But he say this and he give to my hand crush, little crush not for hurt, I know not word.'

'Squeeze. The devil he did. Well, will you leave a note and ask him to ring – um, someone he must talk to at once?' And he gave her a number.

'Thus I do, but I think not this night he come home. He is goned to his works and he leave behind briefcase. I think not he come home for thus is the evil fate of him. Never once yet he leave behind briefcase and I tell – hallo? *Słucham*? … *Ach, to Anglicy, pośpiech, pośpiech, pośpiech.*'

∞

Serena was a nihilist, an honest-to-No-God nihilist. She had nothing in common with those public nuisances the theoretical nihilists – ostentatious sceptics, annoyances at drinks parties. Remember that gleeful old codger, slobbering a little, who told you fee-fi-fo-fummishly that good and evil are delusions? Or the gnarled afflicted creature in a dark poncho who hissed that language is without content? Or that youth, opulently sulky in his expensively-torn jacket, who announced that existence is meaningless? Or – but there's no profit in distinguishing sub-species. It's a simple-minded type. Theoretical nihilists never tire of the thrill of naughtiness. They never suspect the sagging faces of those they address are caused by boredom, not shock; they like to think people back away out of dread. They're content to play at pantomime goblins and would be appalled to discover that there are practical nihilists out there: people like Serena, who have never doubted insignificance.

Obviously, this went far deeper than the wifeyness she'd acquired as a teenager. She had never despaired because it had never occurred to her to hope. She couldn't remember being young enough to believe anything. Ethics, politics, faith, beauty, love, mind, science, law, personality: these seemed to Serena so many fairy-tales, useful only for soothing children afraid of the dark. *Of course* there was nothing beyond her but a swirl of atoms – or not even that: she couldn't take physics seriously, and creditted atoms no more than she creditted causes. There was nothing within her but a brief stutter of pangs and pleasurable quivers, pointless sparks in the abyss; of course.

A real nihilist doesn't mention his conviction, or even formulate it. It never crossed Serena's mind to philosophise. Nonetheless, she lived consistently as any ideologue. About serious things she was intensely frivolous, about trifles she was unaffectedly earnest. Justice was nothing, the belted strap of a handbag everything, since after all the handbag *was*: for an hour or two it was perceived by the void called Serena, before Serena dissolved back into the greater void. It was a true mote, and there is nothing but motes. She herself was a cloud of dust no more than a mote thick, forming a shape that shook and melted a little in the random cosmic breeze. The shape generally pleased her because it was praised, praised by many voices from the void. And that one particular male voice should express possessive pleasure in her form: this was the zenith of what she desired from the infinite zero. She was, in her way, a model wife.

I hope it's clear that Serena wasn't unusually stupid or even, in the usual sense, cold. A certain genteel matiness was part of her equipment, one of the lineaments her nullity assumed. Practical nihilists, who crop up in every climate and civilisation, can make model hostesses, famous courtesans, ardent politicians. Only when you get very close do you detect the stink of the grave. Perhaps that's what Creole mythology is trying to express with zombies.

Serena was trained to be oblivious to many things, especially human character. It took her years to realise what she had married. And even then it was only her imagination that understood. She pictured a meagre meadow, tucked away on a family farm. The landowner's vague as to its whereabouts, wouldn't mind if it were paved over, doesn't really feels he owned it; pays its upkeep doggedly, without concern. That's how Ralph feels about Ralph.

ೞ

Ralph wasn't in the least a nihilist. He had no particular doubts about the world; indeed, he was inclined to superstition. He had no doubts about his own existence. He merely *regretted* existing. He was an absence of an entirely different sort from his wife, a walking bewigged abortion.

His attitude seemed terrible to Serena, who knew that there is no existence to regret. She had no spiritual resilience. Her smooth despair could not endure the proximity of her husband's regrets. Here lying beside her (she felt) was a hole in the air, a whistling gap in the texture of the universe. Of course it wasn't much of a texture; all was thin, tenuous, vacant. But in this locality the universe happened to feel prosperous, almost warm to the touch. There was nothing more to hope for. Why not lie comfortably? Why tear at the sky? Whenever Ralph's harrowed eyes turned to her, freezing winds sucked at her from the beyond, her dusty form threatened to dissolve, she was crazed with vertigo. She endured the terror a zombie must feel in bed with a black hole.

ೞ

Not that Serena could have expressed any of this. But she felt it vividly enough. And the practical result was that in the nineteenth year of marriage she found herself committing adultery every Wednesday afternoon, when she was purportedly playing squash, and most Friday mornings, when she was officially seeing Felicity.

Who was Serena's disgraceful sister, junior by two years although she looked a decade older even on dried-out afternoons. Practical nihilists make very manageable children; already in the nursery Serena's shameless obedience was maddening; in reaction Felicity turned delinquent. She'd done what she could, and it was a lot, to shed her breeding and her bequests. She'd gone through a series of chancer husbands. Ginger, the third, the grossest, owned a chain of strip joints and was no fool. By mismanaging the Ginger divorce Felicity had made herself so poor she had to live way out in Ware, with her four loathsome children by (probably) four different men. Rat, Bat, Fat and Brat is what she called them, although they also had legal names; they were looked after, in a fashion, by a scurrilous *au pair* who kept them locked in their bedroom from sunset to sunrise. Since there were also deadbolts on the front door in case Ginger changed his mind, the house at Ware felt like a fortress as well a prison, and smelt – well, it was noble of Serena to visit such a lost sheep. That is, it would have been noble, if that was where she really was.

As for the lost sheep: she covered for Serena not out of affection, nor even out solidarity, but because she, Serena, was a crashing bore and she, Felicity, was happy to be spared her visits. 'Much better let Nirav have Rena on Fridays.'

As for Nirav Ghosh, he was nothing in particular, nothing at all: a short, chubbyish Bengali, aged twenty-eight and already thinning across his pate, not unlike a wallaby as to feature and stature, born in Wolverhampton and sounded it, interested in computer games and in perilously little beside. He was so hapless that a woman might cherish him with contempt, as certain bad mothers cherish their infants (although as it happens Serena hadn't cherished Tristan at all, he being so much his father's son. She was too wedded to being a glamorous young wife to be much of a mother). Yet if Rena's affair with Nirav wasn't rooted in perverted maternity, it's hard to account for it. Certainly he brought her no great physical pleasure, and not even a social –

 C3

10:04. *Blee blee, blee blee –*

'Good morning, Maltravers Chambers, how can I help you?'

'Good morning. No, goodish morning. Too much snow for "good" don't you think, or don't you?'

'Pardon? Can I help you actually?'

'Might I ask if Sir Ralph Bolswood is in?'

'I can put you through to his secretary.'

'He's there, then?'

'I'm sure he's ever so busy but his secretary can always – hallo? Hall-*oo*? … Bloody time-wasting wanker. God, still twenty-six minutes to smoko. Take me nipples off with sandpaper.'

C3

Nirav wasn't even good for a social thrill. Serena didn't dare show him off, since she had no friends she could trust not to tell Ralph. Even if she'd dared, her friends wouldn't have been thrilled, only contemptuously amused. Certainly in the year of grace 2012 it was in vogue for Q.C.'s wives to whore in Dagenham. But this was 2013, fashion had moved on, that pastime was *passé*; the modish wives of Holland Park were staging affairs with the most brutal policewomen.

'God how things've lightened up since the days of New Labour.'

'Do you *remember*? "Classless solidarity." "Make Britain Young Again." Recycling.'

'The self-righteousness, the *longueurs* …. But *now*. I fancy the Defence Secretary so much I ache.'

'Her librarian twinsets! Her peroxide! Rapture.'

'My W.P.C.'s dyeing her cornrows a crimson unknown to Nature.'

'*Mine* puts glitter nail-varnish on her truncheon. You should see the bruises it produces.'

'Show!'

'…. All right. But tell me if the waiter comes.'

'Good *God!*'

'Cooooo.'

'Bless!'

'Dearhearts, I give you: the golden age of sexual slumming!'

OMNES: 'Slumming!' *Clink-clink-clink, clink, clink.*

'What a shame Serena …' sighed Zoë Moxgrave, if *sigh* is the word. She'd had so much work done, had Zoë, that there was always a fine ambiguity about her tone. Ambiguity was all there was left of her charm, famous when she was young. Now her face was as unwrinkled as money could buy, smooth as a baby's at its open-coffin funeral. Her words, too, came out of her tremendous crimson botox cushions without edge or tone. Zoë herself tried to signal her meanings from her eyes, like one immured in a tower of ivory. But no one attended, fascinated as they were by the splendid tautness of her cheeks. (Ah, but just try kissing them, as many a man and boy and policewoman has – shivering to feel the kiss drop out of nature, drop deep into the abyss of lost time.) Her cheeks were so taut that their unusual tension now, as she pronounced her best friend's name, might have been meant as a pout, or a smirk, a *moue*, a snip, a rueful slackening of her chiselled grin, anything. But let's be generous and say Zoë tried to sigh. 'Serena ….'

'Not Serena, never in a thousand years.'

'So dreary.'

'So *county*.'

'So unadventurous.'

'So *married*.'

Her friends, not guessing how Lady Bolswood's soul was developing, didn't explain to her how to go about slumming. Which is a shame. She might have found herself a more presentable scrap of riffraff than Nirav.

ᳩ

Picture a wedge of brown clay, thin edge pointing down, still moist with mother-milk, its centre fixed by big round eyes inexpressive as a cow's. The clay's been negligently thumbed into shape, enough for us recognise a human face. But it obeys not one precept of beauty, except symmetry: the *ghee*-softened chin and the vague dome of forehead mirror each other. Shave away that lappet of hair, spin the whole upside down, and Nirav's face would have looked just as plausible. Indeed, even his torso might have been twirled about, once we'd flicked off its little tuft of genitals, which resembled green sprouts at the tip of a decaying potato. To look at him, you'd guess Serena had dredged him up from a *balti* restaurant. Which is exactly what had happened.

One evenintg in May she'd been to an *avant-garde* opera about airports called *Carousel of Blood*. This is the sort of misfortune that befalls the wives of the great. The Middle Temple happened to be a patron of the theatre, a brick labyrinth in a fantastically remote corner of Ilford. The building had been, in happier days, a workhouse. At the last moment Ralph couldn't come along and help patronise, so Serena had endured the opera alone for two hours. Afterwards she couldn't face the long ride home without dinner. Anyway (such is the power even of bad art) she found herself churned up within.

Her *balti gosht* wasn't particularly good, but she left a preposterously large tip and – the bravest deed of her life – her mobile number on a torn slip of opera programme, nestled under the tenners.

Serena needn't have been so careful. She wasn't even Nirav's first adventure. He'd already known the extraordinary good fortune of being taken up by a woman better-looking, cleverer and richer than himself. He was just one of those men. It's useless to try to explain. These matters do not go by reason or even taste.

He'd learned what was expected. He returned Serena's calls swiftly. He obeyed her invitations. He smiled a good deal, although Nirav's smiles were never a success: they resembled silent titters, because he couldn't keep his lips still. (Those lips! They were like the lobes of some soft predator rippling in the current, lazily glutting on plankton.) In between grins, he knew to appear pleased with himself, as indeed he would have been if Nirav were philosophical enough to consider Nirav. Women appreciate a certain smugness in their men when their men are dependent.

Dependency was not a burden for Nirav. In time it might have shaded into prostitution. Certainly there was no difficulty for him in cash presents. Honour was preserved because he laid out £11.99 of his takings on an expensive deodorant, shelved behind his usual cheap one and used in preparation for Wednesday afternoons and Friday mornings.

So it had gone on. Then, one Wednesday afternoon in autumn, Nirav suddenly broke up this story, which has so far been a mere comedy of manners of the sourest, most dismal type. He broke it up. It re-formed almost as tragedy.

ଔ

Serena and Nirav were lying in bed getting their breath back (so to speak; neither was self-forgetful enough for anærobic lovemaking), and thinking their thoughts, if we can say that about two people so dim.

The bed was in Nirav's childhood bedroom, in his mother's house, because Serena detested the stink of his bedsit. Mrs Ghosh was prepared to be ordered out of her home sit in to the local café, because Nirav was her only child, and she was a conservative Bengali Hindoo.

Posters for Wolverhampton Wanderers were taped above the bed, where the schoolboy Nirav had put them. Nobody had moved them, which is to say Mrs Ghosh hadn't because she wouldn't dare and Nirav hadn't because he never did the unnecessary. So Serena's eyes rested dolefully on fading yellow-gray thighs and sideburns and mullets. Did anyone really sport moustaches like that, even in 1995? Ralph, she reflected, would be irritated by such ugliness. Not Serena. The urban proletariat was so remote from her she genuinely curious about it.

For one thing to grasp about Serena is that she was much grander than her husband, being only three generations away from proper landed gentry. Her grandmother, wife of a rakish heir, used to tell her about returning at Christmas to Cockwood, the FitzRanulphs' family place. The parish choir would trek up through the park and be given wassail; on Christmas morning the children of the estate would be assembled wide-eyed beneath the tree in the hall, where the family would hand out carefully graduated presents. One year (it was the Abdication Christmas) the maids began sobbing, one after the other, when it was time to sing *God Save the King*. Every Boxing Day the family would put on aprons to serve dinner to the domestic staff. 'I wouldn't like to have been there on Boxing Day, mumsie, it doesn't sound *nice*,' said the infant Serena, returning from a visit to granny, and was scolded by her mother, who'd had exactly the same thought but would have been ashamed to admit it. This calibrates the decay of the family.

'I know the FitzRanulphs are ruined,' Bolswood told himself the afternoon he married Serena, during the speeches to which he did not attend, simply chuckling when everyone chuckled and spinning his glass of riesling round and round in his too-long fingers. He was enduring a moment of unusual clarity, possibly because of the power of the sacrament. Anyway for a few hours the church carry-on elevated and energised his ideas. 'But there's wise blood inside her. As well as a certain courtliness on the outside. If I catalogued her beauty – billows of chestnut hair, fierce or commanding brow, heavy lids on green eyes loose in their sockets, short livid mouth, breasts firm small and separate, bold line of the hips – she'd sound like a common type. The over-ripe harpy. But the fact is, she doesn't look like that at all. The same amount of gilding that vulgarises a bank ennobles a baroque façade. Curves and colours that would cheapen her were she a *bourgeoise* simply emphasise her superb Norman bones. Especially the wide square bone fronting her braincase. How Marius does go on.' Marius was Ralph's head of chambers, wisely selected as best men. 'Under all these pseudo-matey jokes he's really posing the question *Why on earth is Bolswood marrying her?* A possible answer is that, although witless and breasty, her body knows things my body can't.'

For one thing to grasp about Bolswood is that, for all his intellect and wealth, he was a Saxon serf. Intellect and wealth are tenuous. It's flesh that makes us man. Ralph's flesh, although firmed and lengthened by a few generations of dining well, was still the flesh of his *villein* forefathers. His cheeks, palloured by spiritual problems of which we've heard quite enough, were jolly red apple cheeks, genetically speaking. If its public school education had bestowed on it a boney ridge, still the Bolswood nose was designed on the same sensible principle as the turnip. In fact, despite all Jermyn Street could do by way of depilation and perfumery and tailoring, Bolswood's face resembled a pudding. If he'd been allowed to rusticate in the country for a decade or so, his figure too would have relaxed into a wholesome pudding-shape. Jolly tufts would have broken forth, his care-worn moles would have become honest warts. That cunningly-orchestrated yap would have slowed, enriching itself from the soil. The itch of education would have peeled off Ralph, who would almost have have learned to say *Garn*. He'd have been happy and useful as the day is long. No one would be more plausible in an embroidered smock. Day-trippers from Stoke-on-Trent, spying him with his scythe in some flowery-sunny meadow, would have appreciated him as rustic virtue made visible. They would have smiled and waved as they motored past. And reader, *he would have waved back.*

However, as things stood in the world-without-end winter of 2013, Ralph Bolswood remained a fair specimen of the professional classes. That is: his mind was colossal, but its elements were brutal and inhuman. When at last he learned of Nirav's existence he put the boy down as a class-warrior. If commercial motives didn't explain anyone's behaviour, he was inclined to fall back on hatred. Of these three bewildered people, it was Ralph who misunderstood things most drastically.

But let's not be unfair to him. If Nirav was opaque to Ralph's *bourgeois* cleverness, Serena's aristocratic wisdom was almost as useless. When Serena reproached herself, it was along these lines: 'O God, sleeping with a bumpkin! It's barely decent. He'll be boasting to his friends about having a lady.' But Nirav was a postmodern proletarian, with no politics and no friends. Of his acquaintances, some wouldn't credit his account of scoring a rich bird from Up West. The more worldly ones, the ones with jobs, knew such an affair was all too likely, and wouldn't be impressed. So he didn't tell. In any case, it was a lapse of taste in Nirav's circles to let conversation stray far this side of the computer screen. Sex in particular was a matter for videos. Intimacy was to be had second-hand in sites dealing with reality-television celebrities. *Maura feels that at this point in her life Kurt isn't where she's at relation-wise.*

Back in spring, when Serena had taken him away from waitering, Nirav had had no illusions. By autumn he was growing puzzled. The mystery wasn't Serena. What was there in her character to puzzle anyone, even Nirav? It was in himself. He was being moved to break the rules. Or to be less heartless, let's say that human potency (or the Spirit, or the energy of life) flows even through channels as low as Nirav Ghosh. Whatever is human is capable of causeless leaps.

So if this was not a miracle, it was at least an inexplicable incongruity that one November Wednesday afternoon Nirav said: 'I want you to have my babies.'

Serena sat up in bed. It was very fine, her '*What?*' She got the word to ring with *hauteur*, languor, detachment, so that it scarcely sounded like her own voice. In a sense it wasn't. We've examined her personality: there wasn't much there except an anxiety to please men. But she could be startled out of trivial individuality into the broader company of her ancestors. She had within her dregs of feudal dignity. Therefore now she snorted '*What?*' and laughed incredulously, magnificently. Generations of haughty forefathers laughed with her. His babies! This was like being winked at by a stable-boy one's tumbled on hay. The impudence was impossible, nothing could be done with it.

'Oi!' you democratically object. 'What about Nirav's ancestors? Doesn't a yob have as many ancestors as a gent?' So he does. In the harsh days of the Moghuls and in the serene days of the Raj, Nirav's ancestors were Hindoo sharecroppers, every one. They tended jute and rice in the valley of the Ganges until it was time to join their crops in the damp dark warm soil, leaving their place in the sun to children who were just as patient, just as content, just as indebted and bumbling. Ralph's fathers were lucky growing hops beside the Trent, and rose to be yeomen and franklins. Somehow none of Nirav's line ever escaped the orbit of money-lenders. Then came Partition. Nirav's grandfather escaped into exile, but not before he'd seen his family and schoolfellows burned alive by their Muslim neighbours. What descended from him to Mrs Ghosh was a sediment: horror of change. What she passed down to her son was absolute inertia.

This Nirav's heritage was of no use to him. It was a prodigy, uncovenanted by genealogy, breeding or education, that he should have replied to Serena's '*What?*' with: 'I want you to marry me, Belle.'

Not, you will note, 'I want to marry you.' Not even 'I want you to marry me, Rena.' Serena had never been fool enough to let him know who she was, coupling him under the *nom de guerre* Belle. Belle was her pony when she was a girl; the name popped into her head on their first date, if that is the right term for the event, when Nirav asked, with a caution learned in his earlier affair, 'Wha 'm to call you then?', which is subtly different from 'Wha y' called?'

'Belle,' he said now, 'I want you to leave Bennykins.' Bennykins was the name of Serena's brother's shaggy dog when they were children, recalled when she'd first told Nirav of the drunken cruelty of her husband, a hot-blooded broker at Lloyd's. 'Leave Bennykins and come and live with me. I want us to have children.'

Nirav was himself essentially a child, not even a nice one, being selfish, dirty, lazy and disobedient. It was odd for him to desire such a thing as a child of his own. It was odder still that Serena should cease laughing at his desire, put away feudal assurance, and stare down into her lover's wallaby face as if for the first time.

ભ

There'd been a natural slackening of the affair over the summer, while Tristan was home from his last year at Ralph's old school. In October Tristan had gone up – not to Ralph's Oxford college. Thanks to Serena he was more human than his father, but he'd also inherited her brains, and looks, and had to make do with a dubious college in Cambridge.

With her son gone, term-time adultery had resumed on the same weekly schedule. But Serena was half-hearted. The logic of such things should have caused it to fade away as skiing season began.

But at the beginning of November there was a spasm of grace in Nirav, who made his amazing declaration. Having amazed himself with it, he found he couldn't escape it. He kept reiterating that he wanted to live with Serena, to found a family with her; that he loved her; that he needed her. Language like this is heavy, it sinks down from ear to soul, or what passed for soul in Nirav.

There was no cause for such a development. But the fact is, Nirav developed. He grew a bit less squalid. He cleaned out his tiny flat and began to bed Serena there, in what he now thought of as their bed. He made it harder and harder for Serena to view the affair as a caprice with the peasantry.

Snow began in the Alps. Serena said she didn't want to go to Gstaad, preferring to stay in London. Ralph apologetically said he didn't want to go either. Tristan, briefly home for the holidays, went off to Cortina with friends instead.

Christmas came and went, most unlike the Christmases her

grandmother had told her of. In the New Year Serena announced that she was joining a graduate reading group and would henceforth be out late every Tuesday afternoon, adding this to her Friday and Wednesday absences.

In the second week of January Tristan passed back through London on his way way to 'varsity, and brought a blizzard with him. A Russian winter settled on southern England, howling and ravening. There had never been anything like it, or not for generations. The snow seemed inexhaustible, it seemed not to mean to stop. Newspapers made wan jokes about a White Easter. The early lambs were exterminated. Huge lorries careered off dual carriageways into mountainous drifts and were dug out the next morning, the driver dead with a fag heroically frozen to his lip, his trousers unzipped, his *Daily Smear* open to page three over his cold knees.

Holland Park Avenue would grow white, then gray and black as the traffic got to work; briefly white again; on and on; nothing broke the cycle.

'Why does snow attract dirt?' Serena mused one evening, staring desperately out from the bay-window of their drawing room at the rush-hour traffic, working its way between snowbanks dark as coal.

'I'm sorry to say it doesn't,' said Ralph from his armchair, not looking up from his book. 'Dirt's always there. Snow just shows up how nasty things are. Haven't you noticed in the Park? The snow's yellowed by dogs *every few yards*. Urine's always everywhere. So's that black stuff. Working its way into your skin and flesh and' (he said this with real malice, taking a sip of his scotch, not looking up) 'marrow.'

One morning the snow was so deep the 'buses stopped. Serena walked for two hours to be with her lover, bringing him both herself, and a brand of chocolate bar he couldn't do without. The Thames was said to be on the point of freezing over at Westminster, for the first time in two centuries. There was wild talk of frost fairs on the ice. Jokes in the papers gave way to thinkpieces: global warming would bring more winters like this; the English Character must grow more serious with more serious weather. Nirav grew in goodness, a goodness planted, as is often the way, in evil. Serena fantasised about brown babies. Certain grandmothers froze in Poole when heat was cut off to their retirement home, but Ralph brilliantly proved *shall* does not contractually mean *shall* and the case against the gas company collapsed. Serena and Nirav tried to build a snowman, but his hands soon got cold in his gloves, and they had to run inside. Cross-country skiiers reached London from John o' Groats. A sports stadium collapsed in Wales and put a player in a coma; whose sexual exploits Nirav studied over four pages of the *Smear*. Why couldn't he be like that? His affair with Serena had begun as shoddy deception, abrading two selves which were already abraded nearly to the point of facelessness. He was turning it into real, illegal love. From Ben Nevis the view was as far as the North Sea, with nothing in between that wasn't white. Nirav was imperilling our comic tone. He was fashioning what must be washed clean in blood.

iii.

An adulteress resembles a torturer: the essence of the job is hurting someone, but you have a lot of latitude as to how much. *Flay, gut, geld, scorch, behead:* that's only an approximate recipe. It's up to the professional torturer exactly what the victim will feel. Nonetheless, he doesn't want to measure out dollops of excruciation moment by moment. That would be frigid, devillish. Neither does a straying wife. And this is why she's generally found out.

The more Nirav spoke of marriage, the less furtive Serena felt she could be. Thus she didn't always bother showering off Nirav's stink, his twelve quid Spearmint Urban HitMan by Stud. It would be indecent to calculate too exactly: this is how torturers reason.

Every evening except Tuesdays, Ralph came home to his tall Wedgewood-green house on Holland Park Avenue, to his library, his single-barrel malt and his sleek wife in a cocktail dress. 'Darling, you remember we have tickets for the Coliseum? Do you want a drink before you change? We ought to call a cab by six.' She sounded just the same on Wednesdays and Fridays, but on those evenings she smelt of East End wideboy.

A barrister is not going to overlook discrepancies in evidence. In fact he can't. And smells have a cruel habit of lingering in the brain, settling in folds, waiting for some idle moment to erupt. One Friday morning Bolswood, on the way to a meeting in the City, abruptly uttered a choking noise and spilled his legal papers all over the floor of the taxi.

'Y' al' ri' guv?'

'Take … me,' grasped Bolswood, who was suffocating in a cloud of his own subtle sandalwood from Trumpers, 'to … Ware.'

The cabbie's eyes widened in his rearview mirror. 'Where what, guv?'

'To Ware! Up the A10 ….'

Ware's not at its best on dank winter Friday mornings after the last commuter has left. Snowmelt drips from the bogus tiles to the blasted topiary, it drips from the bushes to the low walls of concrete blocks before each house, it slowly works its way into the gutters. There is a sickly quiet, which was particularly dense about Felicity's semi.

There she sat with Clodagh the *au pair* going 'Fuck.' They'd been on a bender last night after Brat, Fat, Bat and Rat were down, and now swayed in wooden chairs by the grubby kitchen table, chain-smoking and suffering.

'Fuck this,' muttered Clodagh; it's up to you how you tackle the name. A pain-filled pause. 'Fuck you.' She often said this of a cold morning. 'Fuck this job. I'm going back to Ballintubber.'

'Don't think you're getting a ticket out of me, worthless bitch. You signed on for the whole fucking year so you're stuck,' remarked the Honourable Felicity FitzRanulph. It's unnerving to think that she was, by definition, as well-born as her sister. Her mascara was pillow-smeared over a patina of blackheads, her blackheads were thick inlaid over dry gray skin; underneath everything was the same fine blood. 'Clear the table. Make coffee.' These were formidable demands. One of the jägermeister empties lay on its side, in a pool of that sticky poison that had become a glue-trap for ciggie butts, smudges of glossy magazine, a violated packet of chocolate digestives. 'It fucking turns my fucking stomach.'

'Fuck that.'

'Aggh!'

'Eeeh!' The door-buzzer made them jump and moan.

'Sss!' went their small black Bat Mog. It was called that because ever since Clod put mogadon in its milk to calm it down – 'The tiniest most harmless sprinkle, really' – it had largely lost the use of its limbs, and liked to lie on its back with its eyes out of focus. It no long purred, it was tremendously silent. Its present noise was the sign of very great surprise. No one called on Fridays until three, when the supermarket van brought cartons of frozen goods for the coming week. With dismay the two bacchantes stared into each other's blighted features.

In justice to Clod, it should be said that most of this ruin dated from innocent childhood in County Mayo, when chickenpox had done its worst. Only recently had her unpocked skin had reared up as acne. Now her face formed a romantic wilderness, sinkholes and startling hillocks with hardly any dull classical plain – 'Ginger!' she hissed.

The buzzer shrilled again, protractedly. Felicity, scion of crusaders and Marcher lords, dared to peer into her hall, choked as it was with huge lightless bits of family furniture.

She'd been childishly grasping when Cockwood was sold. Although she'd carted away far less than what she regarded as her fair share, and allowed Serena to buy her out of some of the biggest things, Cockwood moveables still overwhelmed her poky house, turning it into a sequence of gorges and caverns. The attic was impassable. The upstairs floors sagged. There were bits of a disassembled rosewood four-poster laid along the bannisters. Apart from pale patches where Mog had vomited or Clod had spilled this and that, Felicity's house, wherever one looked, showed acres and acres of grimy varnished wood. It was dark as a fir forest in the Harz Mountains, dark as a mole's lair. 'I fucking hate this clobber,' she'd tell Clod, but short of burning the place down she couldn't think what to do. If an antique dealer had offered her a bottle of spirits per piece, she'd have leapt at it – she'd have thrown in as many ormulu clocks and inlaid frames as his heart desired. But no one offered, for no one guessed what mahogany, oak and teak waited behind her plywood front door, overlaid as it was with acrylic pretending to be cherry veneer.

So now Felicity crept into the dark canyon of her hall to peek from between an art nouveau armoire on its side, and a Gothic hat-stand.

It wasn't Ginger; that was the important thing. It was Ralph's head looming in the panel at the top of her frail front door, silhouetted with snowy light behind, distorted by the pebbled glass so it might have belonged to pantomime demon. Nonetheless she recognised it.

One FitzRanulph had fallen before Sebastopol. Another had carried the standard at Ramillies. A wraith of strategic genius remained with Felicity. She whipped back into the gloom of the kitchen with her finger to her lips.

Too late! The young hag was gone, and presently from the loo arose a tremendous noise. Clod was vomiting with excitement.

'Sorry, Felicity,' came Ralph's large oboe voice, 'it's no good. I can hear you.' He shook the frail door. 'Open.'

The ten seconds it took Felicity's shaking hands to loosen the anti-Ginger chains and bolts are our final ten seconds of peace.

The open door admitted a storm of violence. Not that Ralph struck his sister-in-law. There was no need. The moment she caught wind of his cologne she went to pieces. 'Rena's not here!' she howled, too startled or too malicious to invent a story. 'She's with a man!'

A more self-possessed husband would have nodded and left. But Ralph was faint-hearted, even with a trollop like Felicity. He let her cling gibbering to the snowy forearm of his overcoat. Presently he let her manouevre him – sideways, because of the heaped bookcases and plinths – into the kitchen. The round marquetry table and the William-and-Mary tallboy looked strange on such filthy linoleum. He declined her coffee ('Not instant, no. Sorry'), he refused with a grimace to sit at her table, he stood with folded arms while Felicity's indiscretion overflowed. She betrayed her sister thoroughly, names, dates, sentiments, erotic titbits. 'He gets her to wear opera gloves in bed, likes the classy feel – what do you want, you little shit?' This was to one of the children, Rat, who'd heard Bolswood's voice and crept downstairs.

'Hallo Uncle Ralph,' said Rat, who was called this because he (it was a he) liked to steal into the kitchen for edibles.

'Yes, yes, hallo, um, sorry, Tyron.'

'Okay, you're got your ginger-snaps, now clear off upstairs. This is grown-up talk.'

'Dirty sneaky Rattykins,' added Clod, swiping ineffectually.

'Why can't you keep those little fucks in line? That's what you're paid for .... God it's hell having urchins to care for, now I've gone and lost my train of thought. Anyway here's the bottom line. Nirav's serious. It's not a fling if you know what I mean, it's a – a –'.

'It's mutually empowering,' suggested Clod, who was feeling better for having got those jäegerbombs off her stomach. She knew everything about Nirav. Spiteful gossip about Rena was a staple of Felicity's hangovers. Moreover, Clod was an adept of the human heart: she had an A-level in industrial psych. ('Leastways I would if I'd laid off the fucking white-chocotinis the night before the exam.') 'They're co-dependent but there's authentic synergy.'

'That's it. What Clodagh says.' Felicity's emotional range was narrow. Lust and envy pretty much covered it. Her stock of ideas was also meagre. She was awed by the science of her *au pair*. 'He's totally where she's centred.'

As for Clod, although she enjoyed showing off, what she really craved was the unseemly scene. Sir Ralph's reserve had frightened her in the past. Might he be goaded now? 'They self-actualise,' she crooned, moistening her upper lip with her large gray tongue. 'They're no-way commitmo-phobic.'

'Exactly. He wants to do the decent and tie the knot.'

Ralph scarcely attended. He wasn't reached by anything these sluts could say. The horrid little house was empty of his wife: he knew it the instant Felicity swung back the door (it had felt like unscrewing the porthole of a spaceship). Here was an emptiness so immense it sucked away everything he possessed. His life was emptied of her. He'd become nothing more than an impediment to his wife's decency, to her wifeness; a blot in the sunlight, an apology for a man, a sorry specimen.

It would be a mistake to calibrate Ralph's love according to this sudden despair. Love had little to do with his sick feeling. A man with such a tenuous hold on himself requires exteriors. Bolswood cherished his house, practice, knighthood and county-family wife not because they comforted him, but because they made him visible to others and to himself. Now his cladding had fallen away. It was as bad as being disbarred. Serena had killed him.

His poker-face had been exercised in court for thirty years. He let none of his anguish show. For a few minutes he played the gruff undeceived husband. He gnawed his lip, scrunched his fist, pacing about the filthy little kitchen – treading on the tail of Mog, who convulsed a little – and made his sister-in-law promise not to let Serena know of his visit. She promised. Then he farewelled her with a terse nod, worked his way through her heaped antiques, and shut the door behind him, too gently to rattle the pane.

Felicity was abashed. 'He took it like a man.'

Clod, bilked of an exciting scene, sniffed 'Auto-narcissistic denialism.'

'Ssss.'

'She told on Auntie Rena. She told on her,' Rat was saying to Fat, Bat and Brat upstairs, as they worked their way through the gingersnaps. In that guilty household the one rule was never to tell. Do as you will and never speak what's done.

There's something to be said for this code

⚃

That evening Serena was, as they say in melodramas, radiant, meeting her husband at Le Gavroche. How poised she seemed to him, how graceful in manner. How incredible that she faintly stank of Urban HitMan.

Ralph struck her Serena preoccupied and apologetic, but no worse than always. She greeted him with the usual peck.

He led her to a good table. 'And how was Felicity this morning?'

'Oh, you know,' said Serena, furrowing her brow over her menu.

She was not affecting to study it to evade Ralph's eye. She was giving it sober attention because she took victuals seriously. All her ancestors had. (Her sister, alas, did not.) The soul of Serena Bolswood was parched, but soul was a miniscule part of her; like her husband she was essentially a body; her flesh exuded a sort of corporeal halo. Grandeur hung about this trumpery jade, the sheen of centuries of luxurious grub. The waiter had noticed at once, and hovered behind her chair. 'Felicity? As ever. Why don't they have lobster mousse any more?' The waiter bent over her, murmuring gravely, reverently. 'You could? How tremendously good of you.' He bowed gallantly and trotted off to the kitchens, a champion on a quest, proud to strive for such a lady. Serena, tranquil-faced, put down the menu and folded her hands over it, a nun with a breviary. 'It was a depressing visit, Ralphie. It's pitiful how that pimply Irish teenager drags Fel down.'

'Ah,' said Ralph. This how it was to be, then. The damage Serena had inflicted on him was what any conscientious torturer might inflict without noticing, heated irons being so sharp, eyeballs so frail; and he was fantastically good at hiding torture. Their evening passed calmly.

And the next. And the next. Violence raged away in the depths of him, but he was an enclosed person. So was she. They smiled slightly at each other as across a canyon. This was how it was, and who knows how long the false peace might have lasted if the witches of Ware hadn't tired of it, and nudged on the catastrophe?

℞

It took a week for Clod to wear down Felicity's caution. On the last day of February she prevailed, during a fluffy duck hangover. (A fluffy duck, reader, is equal parts egg-yolk liqueur and white rum beneath a blanket of heavy cream.) Felicity, who was feeling too unwell to worry about her promise to Ralph, telephoned Holland Park, and betrayed her betrayal. 'He was awful, Rena. Threatening.'

'You had the children to think of', mouthed Clod across the kitchen table.

'I had the children to think of. I had no choice. I had to tell.'

Serena, who had making herself a salad for lunch, a new recipe involving unpeeled beetroot, was shattered. 'Fel! O God, *no*! ... Who could've guessed he *knew*?'

'You should have seen him, Rena. He sobbed and sobbed. Shrivelled up and sank through the floor.' Clod gave Felicity a double thumbs-up.

'How can I face him?'

Clod mimed twisting a knife. Felicity – who'd have guessed a FitzRanulph could grow so coarse? – said: 'Well watch how you go girl and he'll never know you know he knows, you know? You can still keep it under the bed if you see what I mean', and rang off before Rena could hear her cackling with her minion.

Serena did see what she meant. For some minutes she fluttered about her huge house like a moth in lampshade, distractedly opening and shutting doors, uttering little whinnies, biting the skin on the back of her hand, slamming her palms on the banisters and shouting blasphemies. (It was Łucja's day off.) But this phase didn't last. Serena was sprung from a line of magnates used to committing adultery in hovels on their estates, and also used to putting such adulteries behind them. Each of them had returned in due season to Cockwood and to its current *châtelaine*. That is why their lands remained theirs; that is how their line continued; that is why Serena existed. Managing adultery was part of her essence.

Thus, while it would be fatuous to say that she loved her husband, it misses the point to say she plotted to keep him merely out of fear. She had floated into Sir Ralph's keeping because she was a piece of fluff. She wafted into the arms of Master Ghosh for the same reason. But fluffiness was only individual, and we've seen how frail her personality was. In November her virile ancestors had over-ruled it, commanding her to fall in love with her paramour. Now, in March, they over-ruled her again, commanding it to stop being in love. Once more she obeyed.

Her spasm of panic passed off. She began telling herself 'This is an opportunity.' And 'I have to get a grip on things. I've been drifting into such danger.' She didn't mean the scandal of divorce. Divorce, if it came, she would manage; she was not Felicity. The peril was of a change of man. Imagine exchanging Ralph, who represented normality even if he repulsed her, for a shop-boy, standing for she couldn't think what. That was unthinkable. If wasn't what she was.

Dozens of FitzRanulphs before her had triumphed on such occasions. Dozens of times a FitzRanulph had had occasion to speak sadly but firmly to a dairy-maid whose maidenhead he'd filched, or to the daughter of a tenant he'd debauched, or to the merry widow of a neighbour. 'My family honour, which happens to incorporate virtue, trumps our love, which happens to involve vice.' 'Here we go Betty my good girl, here's six gold sovereigns and we'll say no more about it'.

'Madam, enough, *adieu*.' '*Je donne la amur duz voz, ma damozel*.' Serena feels that at this point in her life Nirav isn't where she's at relationship-wise. This would be one more victory for the dynastic principle. Serena would shake off her dangerous liaison because she could. She had self-sufficiency, a gift from outside her self, just as her husband's magnificent voice was outside his self. It was hers as arbitrarily as a bequest from a cousin she'd never met.

She tidied her hair and went back to building her salad. Her ancestors relaxed their attention. She relapsed into cowardice and began hedging her resolution with provisos. 'I'm not exactly breaking with Nirav. Not necessarily. I'm simply going to stop him being so awfully serious about it all. Yes. I'm not going to be so serious myself, either. Most of all, I'm going to stop Ralph taking it so seriously. We can come to an understanding. There.' She felt rather sophisticated. The beetroot salad was a success.

 og

I'm not sure Serena was wrong as a matter of fact. Both her men were weak as water, and God knows what they might have put up with. Bolswood was just the material from which *maris complaisants* are made. With a little discouragement Ghosh might have slipped back into the gigolohood intended for him by fallen Nature. She might not have had to choose.

However, any scheme for not taking love seriously has to be spelled out. If she'd dictated it to both men at once, she'd have saved both a lot of discomfort. But the thought of putting her cosmopolitan idea to Ralph, or even Nirav, caused a collapse in her morale. Muddle grew in her head; and this inevitably turned into an impulse to bolt.

'I'm going away,' she told herself as soon as her bloody-looking salad was finished, 'going at once. Breathing space. When I get back we'll arrange things. We all need breathing space. How long before R. returns? An hour? An hour. The green Vuitton bag. The long suede overcoat and fox-fur cap. No. The velvet cloche. No. Fur cap. I can do it.'

She did it. Fifty-eight minutes later Ralph got home to found his wife gone and, on the big Burmese table in the hall, propped against the jade vase, a note. There was a slip in it, which of course he noticed. Slips are the nuisance of writing quickly. A writer who is insincere must take her time.

Darling R: you remember you promised me a Tuscan holiday as a fortieth birthday present? Well I know you'll be too busy to get away until the Murchison case is finished so I'm taking it now on impulse alone. It's the snow: I can't bear all this dirt in the snow. I just need a little breathing space from the snow. EasyJet are offering wonderful specials. It took me ten minutes to buy my ticket and fifteen minutes to pack!!! I'll be back in a week, or so, behave yourself darling, I'll bring you some majolica. I love very much.
    S.

&#x03;

Serena's idea of Ralph's idea of behaving himself was to find himself a girlfriend. Zoë's mask-face flickered through her imagination. How foul to hear cries of ecstasy emerging from that! Oh well, Ralph might not mind. *Quid pro quo.* It's how these things work themselves out. After the breathing space, when she got back from Florence, the Bolswoods would tacitly reconfigure themselves as a mature couple. The complaisant stage of marriage was much practised in Holland Park, and much admired. The Moxgraves, for instance: Zoë was never home because a face that expensive couldn't be wasted on the nanny, and Hugh, lest he behold the face, spent nights and dawns in chambers, working so hard he was sure to be called to the Bench. Perhaps Ralph wouldn't even need a girlfriend. Perhaps under the new dispensation he too would make work his mistress. This happy thought carried Serena through the squalor of Luton and onto her 'plane.

However, Ralph's idea of behaving was to destroy himself leaving no trace. He saw at once, reading Serena's note, that she knew he knew. For a moment the violence seething within him surged in the direction of Ware. 'Untrustworthy bint! Damn her! Damn her murky shack. Damn that everlasting fug of cheap cigarettes' (at present masked by the aroma of regurgitated fluffy duck.) But the impulse of revenge died away. To what end, to what end? He'd forseeen, a week ago at Le Gavroche, that Serena would soon find out that he knew. Why trouble Felicity? What would be the point? She didn't matter. No, it was clear where his violence should be directed. Now it was time for him to go, to go absolutely, go out and never be found.

ଔ

That was Friday. He'd spent the weekend planning his departure; now it was Tuesday evening; here he was in his baseball cap; here was High Wycombe. It was time to perform the manouevre of changing carriage.

In the new carriage everyone was reading newspapers. He considered the newspapers: 'I don't think they'll report me as suicide. They'll postulate an act of random thuggery. Out of deference to the Bar, or to spice up editorials on crime. I'll be something for the Press to smack its lips over.' He peered out the window. The blizzard was worse than in London. Cascading newsprint. Smacking white-fall, pressing down. 'Of course Serena'll understand what's happened .... What'll her face look like when Łucja rings her in Florence?' He imagined this conversation: '"For four days, lady, four whole days, Sir Bolswood no come home. I fear he is goned. The police I have told thus also." Serena never looks as handsome as when she's digesting bad news.' He pictured her at the funeral, in the charcoal she found more becoming than blatant black. 'A model widow. A model of *chic* grief. If there are press photographers she'll be careful to cling to Zoë Moxgrave. She knows how radiant her face looks set beside that painted plastic....' Bolswood's imagination, for want of better work, slithered sideways from Serena to the Moxgrave. 'Her hair! Despite the peroxide, it's more alive than her skin. It's a human thing, painfully fixed on the inhuman geometry of her forehead. Yes, impaled. And her loins: *can* they be blank and tight as her forehead? Can they?' Then he remembered what he was about, and shook off such thoughts. 'Serena won't tell Tristan. Even Felicity won't be cruel enough to do that. I think.... No, not even Felicity. For Tristan my disappearance will be clean. Insoluble. Uncertainty will blur his grief. *Will* Tristan grieve, exactly? He'll regret. Pine, sorrow. A month, and the police will discreetly abandon their enquiries. Seven years and I'll be declared legally dead. Meanwhile Tristan's allowance is settled. And the Trust can pay out even before a decree of death *in absentia*. Yes, it's neat. It's as it should be.' He forced himself to put doubt away. He was glad, damn it, glad to be on this train, glad to be vanishing, untraceably as a snowflake, into the snowy depths of England, closing about him blank and tight as a tunnel.

ଔ

17:06. *Blee blee –*

'Good afternoon, evening almost, Maltravers Chambers, how can I help you?'

'Hallo, Angela. Serena here.'

'Lady Bolswood! It sounds like you're next door. Bet it's ever so much warmer in Italy than it is here.'

'Lots of sun, but a chill off the hills after sunset. Would you put me through to the great man?'

'He's long gone I'm afraid, Lady Bolswood. Packed up and left nearly two hours back.'

'*Really?* It can only be, what, five o'clock there.'

'Well he slacks off when you're not here to keep an eye!'

'I suppose so. How odd. Where was – . Well, it was only to say – no, don't worry, I'll try him at home. Perhaps. Thanks Angela. Good-bye!'

'Bye-bye then Lady B.! Bring me back a handsome Italian! Bye! …. Fuck me with a cheese-grater, the bitch sounded shifty. What's it all about, then? Twenty-two minutes to home-time.'

☙

The Guilty Party was 'phoning from Florence, where she was buying trinkets for Nirav and substantial antique majolica for Ralph. It's typical of Serena's set of mind that although she was happy to shop for them both at the same time, *pudeur* required her to stow the presents in separate bags. Now she rang off, sniffed, and dropped her mobile 'phone into a bag (the lover bag, significantly, not the husband bag). Serena was aware that she had not kept irritation and suspicion out of her voice; Angela Flank was a terrible gossip.

But where *was* the wretch going in the middle of the afternoon? He never left chambers early. Was there some floosy? Was he with Zoë already?

After a few minutes, and the purchase of a Michelangelo's *David* snow-globe, Serena calmed herself. It was silly to be jealous. If they were going to open their marriage, she had to affect a certain chumminess with Ralph over his adventures. 'So where have you been, *mon vieux?* Off shagging in the suburbs?'

But it was all nonsense about floosies. Not Ralphie. She ought to speak to him. He must be home by now. Where else did he have to go?

☙

17:11. *Ka-ring ka-ring. Ka-ring ka-ring.*

"He's *pretending* to be out," said Serena through her teeth.

Ka-ring ka-ring, ka-ring ka-ring, ka-ring ka-ring, ka-ring ka-ring.

ᘓ

Ralph was not pretending. At that instant he was leaving the train at Saunderton, his terminus. ('That word!') The blizzard had twisted sideways. It made the platform a mere amorphous swirl, an abstract canvas, white dashes on black. The glowing waiting room was a submarine on the floor of a stormy ocean. The other two passengers who got off at Saunderton – one thin and jaunty and pale, one quite opposite, short and chubby and shambling and dark; symbols of something – pulled their hats over their faces and vanished moaning toward that glow. Bolswood let them go past, standing behind a column. He needed, for the last time, to be invisible.

When thinking through his disappearance, this was the moment that worried him most. The idea was to wait for the platform at Saunderton to be clear. Then he'd slip away, not through the station building but out the small exit that led past the sheds, over a stile, and into the woods. He had studied aerial photographs on his iPad; he had rehearsed his shamble, not too fast, as he cleared the fence; thus, thus, he would part company with his species. But it's impossible not to be conspicuous if you go for a woodland stroll in a blizzard, no matter how common your overcoat, how forgettable your cap. He dreaded the curious glance of some commuter, or some clerk with too little to think about. 'Hallo? I'm telephoning to report that I have seen Sir Ralph Bolswood's photograph on my television and did notice a man of that description detraining the delayed 16:56 on Tuesday. What, Constable? Oh indeed I'm certain, for I observed him entering the woods in the anterior of the station. Yes, I would describe his manner as suspicious.' 'Thank you, sir. – Right, lads, we've had a sighting of the missing barrister. Bledlow Great Wood. Gary, telephone Swindon for body-sniffing dogs.' And what can he do about it? Nothing but hope that whatever watches over suicides (perhaps it is indeed Nothing) will watch over him, staying all other watchers –

ᘓ

17:28. *Ka-ring* – what? You again, is it? Ring on, Lady Bolswood! Trifle with your iPhone! Would you were wringing your hands. Would you might indeed speak to your husband. But he expects no voice to reach him again, not now. He has passed to a lonelier, darker place than your light mind comprehends, where you have not been nor can go: into fell wilderness, slaying from very purity. What though it be but a corner of Buckinghamshire? For him it is the vestibule of the void. What he seeks up that icy track is the gate of hell. Behold, Lady Bolswood, how swiftly he seeks it!

It's half past five when he leaves Saunderton station. He is in luck. No one seems to see him. The snow suddenly stops. No sun comes out, but the later afternoon sky reappears, heavy, bruised and pregnant with more snow. The air is clear but twilit.

Such is the egotism of suicides, even diffident ones, that he imagines the storm has stopped for him. The stage is set and now we await the action, such as it is. The naked trees close in about him, their silence absolute. He feels half-buried already.

It's fully two miles from Saunderton to the place ordained, but he takes his *via dolorosa* at full-tilt and seems likely to be finished before dusk. Everything is smothered in whiteness, all turnings look alike, but although sometimes he sinks to his thighs, and wades through the drifts (not like the Lapp princess in the story), he does not slacken. He swings his legs outward, spinning them almost like wheels. He sprays snow up into the twilight in the fury of his advance.

He does not err, he does not lose the ancient road. Here the track forks, as he knew it would.

Here it runs parallel to itself, broadly in a ditch (a mere treacherous furrow, now, in the white smoothness), narrowly atop the right bank.

The wire fence, yes.

The kissing gate, where he'd expected it.

And here (as in any Gothic penny-dreadful; a bass tremor on the organ, please) is the looming alder with a double trunk, overlooking his resting place. He pauses at last, to get his breath back before losing it forever, and gazes up at the alder. The one time he was here before was in spring, and the thing was in full leaf. Now it's bare, so comparisons are hard. But he really thinks it's grown a lot in the twenty-five years since he last came along the Icknield Way.

CHAPTER 2
The Icknield Way

i.

'*The Icknield Way is the most ancient road in Britain. The Iceni traded amber along it before the Romans came, hides, slaves and hunting-dogs; and even then it was old. The Molmutine Laws of King Dunvallo, said to derive from the code brought to our land by the Trojans, mentioned the road and protected it* maxime autem, *which is as much as to say, above all things. St Edward the Confessor made the lofty gesture – '.*

'Sorry, I'm finding this a bit florid for a guidebook.'

'And you, Ralphie, are generally found a bit arid for an undergraduate. Hush. *The Confessor made the lofty gesture of placing the whole Icknield Way under the King's Peace. Bouts of the Civil War were fought up and down it....*'

'Slay the Roundheads,' bellowed Will Rawleigh merrily, 'slay them!'

'Is he,' asked Bolswood, troubled, 'going to shout the whole way?' Rawleigh was leaping about ahead of the other two, thwacking at the sunny hedges with a stick.

'He is,' sighed Spurdle. He wore a sleepy, faraway smile; he was holding his book open as he walked. 'The benighted idiot is.'

'Two miles gone!' shouted Rawleigh. Thwack, thwack. 'Tally ho! A hundred and fifteen to go! Yoiks!'

Spurdle had been Rawleigh's disciple since prep school, assigned the role of jeering at his master. For Rawleigh, who was no fool, knew himself to need watching. He was red-headed, red-and-white-skinned, broad and boisterous; would certainly be handsomely fat in middle-age; might also be a swaggart and a buffoon, as were a number of his uncles. So far, at twenty, he was merely fleshy and robust. His enthusiasms came and went fast enough to be ridiculous, but he was not himself ridiculous, or not yet. He didn't resented being repressed; since he was in danger of being raucous, it was clearly other people's business to repress him. This is an exasperating attitude. But the people he exasperated were far less important than the ones he made happy. Spurdle, for instance, would have become merely bookish without Rawleigh's puppyish bouncing.

As to the rest, the two of them were in complete earnest about the estates they were going to inherit, Spurdle in Banffshire and Rawleigh in Cumberland. Their preposterous old-fashioned names were dear to them. Spurdle wore sleeveless Argyle jumpers and tweed suits, although he drew the line at pipes. Rawleigh never thought about clothes, and turned up at university with heaps of his father's suits and jumpers. Both unaffectedly enjoyed long walks. They were chivalrous and reticent, or to put it another way, their attitudes to tenants, women, animals, God, foreigners and themselves were splendidly antique.

None of this was a pose. They weren't even reacting against anything. The damnable twentieth century had simply passed their families by. True, one of Rawleigh's great-aunts had run off to London to be a suffragette, was gaoled for arson and force-fed in Holloway; while Spurdle's grandfather had at one time sympathised with Oswald Mosley. But by and large the Rawleighs and Spurdles (especially the Spurdles) had declined to take seriously anything that happened after 1914. They weren't yokels; the Rawleighs weren't even Tories. Sons and daughters of both families went off to boarding schools and universities, grand tours and wars. They read about it our civilisation's misadventures. But country sport and landlord duty bounded their horizons. The twentieth century's doings – metaphysical despair, sensationalist art, wild mores, political fanaticism, massacres – sounded to them as quaint as the antics of Arabian tribes. The two youths grew up in an atmosphere not so different than it had been under the Stuarts. Their houses were a bit more decrepit, the heating slightly better, the clothes much more drab; that was all.

In most ages, before or since, they'd have seemed rather ordinary squires' sons. Now – it was May 1988 – there happened to be a great dearth at Oxford, and the two of them were making a tremendous impression. They were discussed in *Cherwell*; they were imitated by the spiritually-famished children of merchant bankers or Social Democratic M.P.s.

Rawleigh and Spurdle didn't notice this mild *cultus*. They wouldn't have understood it if they'd noticed it, and wouldn't have cared much if they'd understood. It wasn't, after all, that they had much to offer. They just didn't have the middle-class diseases (anxiety, thinness of soul, self-consciousness, paralysis of good taste), and were not bewildered by the sudden end of Europe's collectivist nightmare. Collectivism had never made much impression in Cumberland or Banff. They demonstrated man's extreme liberty as a species *not* to be moved, not to be spun in revolutions. The two of them were nearly outside history, like animals or geological formations, and their power, being innocent, worked by being blind to itself.

It so happened that Rawleigh and Spurdle were spending a week of May walking the length of the Icknield Way, from Knettishall Heath ('A fine name,' said Spurdle, peering at the map) to Ivinghoe Beacon. ('Even finer!' shouted Rawleigh, 'is there something there we can burn?') They often went walking together; this time, as an experiment, they had taken with them a third fellow, a glum clever bloke from Spurdle's college. Afterwards they voted his presence only a mixed success. But as long as the Icknield walk lasted, Rawleigh and Spurdle were pleasant enough to Ralphie Bolswood, who was their guest.

Bolswood found that week intoxicating, not because people were generally rude to him – no one ever was, that was part of his problem – but because for as long as the trek lasted, his own personality was absorbed. Young Bolswood's inner predicament, as we have seen, went deeper than the usual upper-middle-class predicament: he loathed existing. Dring that week he discovered what it meant to be part of a party, and ceased to be hag-ridden because he largely ceased to be. He didn't admire Spurdle, and was irritated by Rawleigh. But for a week their exuberance bounced him out of himself. The party sang rugby songs much of the way, it drank phenomenal amounts of ale which did not slow it down, and it demonstrated that, when covering a dozen miles a day, it's possible to eat a leg of lamb in a pub at lunch, and another leg of another lamb at another pub at dinner, and like it.

Unthinking exuberance will no doubt remain with Spurdle and Rawleigh until they die. It didn't outlast the week for Bolswood. He wasn't a man who could escape outward into love, and reached the age of fifty-five without having a friend. Nor could he escape inward into creativity; nor could he escape upward into humility. He was incapable alike of affection, art or the contemplation of God. But there's a fourth way out of the tortured self, a route dangerous and indeed (as in this case) likely to be fatal. That's the route Bolswood discovered, walking down the Icknield Way.

ରେ

Long-legged Spurdle read aloud from county guides as they walked. He could step unerringly over huge roots corrugating paths and ford streams without looking up from the page. It was a small obscure prowess, but his own. We've heard him reading about the Civil War as they left the heath called Knettishall. A minute later, unerringly mounting a stile, he turned a few pages and pronounced: 'It'll be all chalk.'

'Sorry – what will?'

'The ground, you decadent townie. Our whole route runs over chalk except for a bit near Chrishall where we'll be crossing glacial boulder clay.'

'Bring back the glaciers, bring back the glaciers! God, can't you just picture those lovely glittering blighters grinding their way back down from Greenland? Glory glory hallelujah! Sawing mountains in two, freezing seas dry, rolling hills flat as if they were pastry, knocking over – this heath doesn't look like chalk. Observe the Scots Pine and gorse. Spurdle, you lie.'

'*Around Thetford gravels, masking the chalk, shape the unusually dry expanse known as the Brecks.*'

'Ah. Spurdle, you lie not.'

'*But after that the country of the Way remains open, with the texture of its soils light, for they –*'.

'Look at that pine over there, poor bastard, scrawny and twisted as a Jesuit. Sinister name, Brecks, and I don't hold with gravel, it's not sporting for greenery to have everything drained out of it like that. Bet the humans round here are dry buggers, too.'

'*For they –*'.

'Our place is all marlstone and we're princes among men. Silt can produce a gentleman, loam certainly, clay, sand, I have my doubts about limestone, peat yes, chalk always; but gravel breeds rebels and cowards and –'.

'Rawleigh, silence. *For they sit either on a sandy bed covering the chalk, or on the chalk itself.*'

'It's like wine-tasting notes,' mumbled Bolswood, shaking his head. The other two, children of gentlemen farmers, were used to reading the land around them. Ralph had never thought of savouring anything that wasn't human, except for claret. He was a cultivated youth, but a child of cities and institutions, hungry for scholarships; what was below the level of intellect was raw material for pleasure or work. *Nature* was a greenish waste, usually wet, flickering past between towns. Some pages back we imagined an Edwardian peasant idyll for Bolswood. If that had come to pass, he too would have known the land as fellow-creature and workmate. But he never planted, harvested, bred or hunted.

That May, as they walked over the rounded breast of middle England, he was overwhelmed by a certain idea of land. It was older idea than anything in Rawleigh's head, or Spurdle's. Bolswood did not discover the land as a friend, but as a devouring presence. The inhuman world was not just more beautiful than humanity, it was stronger. Its tendrils tugged apart mortar. It overgrew thought. It was indifferent to mind although incomparably more subtle. It waited, it prevailed, it ran through and around all things, it was maternal, it was hostile. And Ralph exulted in it.

Thus when Spurdle read '*The Icknield Way loves to cleave the flank of high ground, for the summit of clay ridges is often topped with damp, yielding clay*', Rawleigh shouted 'Mucky place, England, mucky!'; but Bolswood pictured the hills, wonderful in arrogance, crowning themselves with a clay diadem man could not transverse.

Hills aloof! Earth unthinkably more ancient than any road or people! Divine and yielding mud, trampling the Icknield Way into the chalk! *Laudamus te,* mud, *adoramus te,* mud, *gratias agimus tibi propter magnam gloriam tuam!*

The boys slept in the upper rooms of inns. Rawleigh snored as if conducting a debate with himself, Spurdle was silent and remote. Bolswood was insomniac, but ecstatically so. He watched moonshadows manouevre themselves over beams and plaster. He listened to night-noise of owl and fox, thinking *Man is a tedious fungus on the bark of the world* – which was, obviously, a more comforting notion than thinking of Ralph Bolswood as a fungus.

He'd think: *The complexity of the ground is as great as the complexity of the sad brains walking over it on two legs.*

He'd think: *Spurdle over there; with all his serenity what does he know?* He'd think (remember he was young and lonely, and bound to be pompous): *The Iceni knew better than we do. They went along their Way in fear of the Powers. They dropped silver cups down wells in honour of Blodeuwedd and Dôn. And the refugees from Troy! They must have come this way too, sacrificing on the flanks of these hills to Aphrodite.* But then he remembered the Molmutine codex, and laughed to himself, and slept.

The next morning they passed the Colne. That night Bolswood made himself too drunk to sleep with the thought of Earth. *Terrible in her beauty. Almost eternal. Present before thinking began, present even before the gods and goddesses, fated to outlive thinking too. What does goodness matter? Or law?* This from his college's Scholar in Jurisprudence! *How can any system matter? Each thought sinks back into the breast of the Mother, putrefies in her fecundity, vanishes. Before all things waits her wordless cruelty and loveliness.*

Thus thought Ralph Bolswood night after night, escaping the bleak, stale misery of his usual thoughts downward. Thus he made himself pagan.

☙

By day the boys felt so vigorous they weren't satisfied merely walking the Way. If they saw anything interesting on either hand they swerved. And on the third day Bolswood lifted up his eyes and saw the place, a splendid hill, the final rampart of the Chilterns, looming over them on their left.

Like everything in England, the scale of the Chilterns is mellow; a barbarian from Russia or America would say *small.* But all things are relative to human imagination, and seen from below, up a chalk path, the Chiltern scarp rears dramatically as an Alp.

Singing they ascended the sublime height of Wain Hill. The Vale of Aylesbury opened before them. Their final chorus ('The drip, drip, drip of the syphilitic prick of a British Grenadier!') woke from the trees a murmuration of starlings; the boys laughed, and entered the shade of a beech forest. Spurdle, as always, had his guide open. 'This is called, um, Bledlow Great Wood … *Bledlow* means *bloody hill*: there was a bloody great battle here between Anglo-Saxons and heathen Danes –'

'Who won?'

'Doesn't say. *In* –'.

'Bloody cheek. Bled cheek.'

'In 1350 –'.

'Bled Danes, invading our country, taking our women, bledding our lows.'

'In –'.

'Kill all Danes, kill all Danes!'

'I'm sorry – not Brigitte Nielsen,' put in Ralphie, shyly; he was known to have a thing for this actress.

'Kill all Danes except Brigitte Nielsen, kill all Danes except Brigitte Nielsen!'

'In 1350', persevered Spurdle, '*the Benedictines of Luffield Priory modified a phallic symbol, cut into the chalk of Bledlow Great Wood long before to mark the Icknield Way. The famous Bledlow Cross occupies a small clearing of broadleaf woodland looking nor'-northwest, visible from the B4009, and may be –*'

'Bloody monks, invading our clearings, stopping us taking our women, modifying our phalluses.'

'Crossing each *T*, dotting each *I*, finishing us,' sighed Spurdle.

'What're you saying?' Rawleigh was suspicious of Spurdle's asides, because his friend had recently become a papist and had to be watched for infected thought, especially in his jokes.

'*The Cross may be reached by ascending an eroded cutting for two hundred yards off the bridleway.* Which must be that turn-off up there,' shoving his guidebook into his knapsack. 'Shall we go and see?'

They did, and found it a shoddy piece of work, essentially loose bits of chalky soil strewn within a shallow trench seventy feet long, overdue for repair. 'Sorry to say it,' said Bolswood, 'but it wouldn't have looked like a phallus even when it was a phallus', which was true.

Yet undeniably (thought Bolswood) the blobby shape made a difference. It made the flowery clearing feel solemn.

The other boys thought so too, but didn't like to say. *A cut cross, a hill of sacrifice*, mused Spurdle, *Moriah; life-death*, and his mind spun up into the blue vault of contemplation. '

What fuckwit carves a seventy-foot anything just to point a road? thought Rawleigh in his hearty way. *No, I bet the Iceni put it here to celebrate abominable things*, and he conjured up a rite in this grove: midnight, a bonfire, Druids crowned with mistletoe, the victim bound and naked but for woad, a slit made in his belly, his entrails teased out and nailed to that sacred oak; then he's whipped round the trunk, wrapping it in guts like a windlass, until he falls and the haruspex stoops to read the future in his convulsions. Rawleigh pictured this horror with such gusto that, boy that he was, he delighted and dismayed himself at the same time. He twitched his head about as if to sniff up the taint of ancient blood.

Meanwhile Bolswood was lost in the thought, not of the cutting, but of the stuff cut: chalk chopped from the soft bones of our planet. From the Mother ....

'Ale!' bellowed Rawleigh. 'Not here! Into the woods! Ale! Shade! Ale!' The afternoon was by English standards hot. It had become a tradition over the last few days that, halfway between bouts of roast lamb, they should stop for bottled beer, cheese and pears. They plunged into the shadow of the high trees, bounding and shouting 'Along here!' and 'No – off to the right', terrifying the wildlife for miles around. Tending from the path, they found ground more broken and more ribbed. And then suddenly they were among bluebells.

If you think bluebells are pretty things you have never got on your knees among them to marvel, as Ralph did now. *'Only bluebells survive the darkness and coolness beneath the cathedral vaults of beech, so common in Buckinghamshire,'* read Spurdle, standing over him and eyeing him askance. *'Only bluebells can pierce the heavy leaf-drift. They kill off dog's mercury and other – '*

'They're wild critters, wildflowers,' shouted Rawleigh, who was bounding on ahead, vanishing into the trees. 'Slaughter, slaughter, slaughter. Here! Come down here.'

Ralph the pagan was worshipping their vigour, worshipping the haughty glory of their shape: the hanging bells, half-a-dozen or a dozen thick on one side of the stem, which curled with its splendid weight. When he moved his hand the carpet of flowers shook at him, the stems nodded, the bells silently tolled for him. He drew his fingers through the bluebells and snagged them on the bold rims, curled back in tapering tongues; his fingers prickled from their aweful baptism in dew. There was the faintest noise as the stems clicked back and forth, majestically, as if the floor of the forest were itself the canopy of a forest for ants; he buried his face in the mass of them, tasted sweet gum and smelt subdued honey. And the colour! Here purple as merlot grapes, here dark blue as the southern sea at dusk, here exactly the same shade as the sky. Moony colours. Colours from beyond the circles of earth. Ponds of blueness not wetness. The Great Mother gouging holes in the stuff of herself, revealing sky below as well as above. The world floats in a blue womb ....

Ralph rose, stupefied. He followed the noise of Rawleigh, and found himself dropping into a dell or miniature gorge. A long thin streak of bluebells, like a runner-carpet down an hotel corridor, marked the edge of the damper ground above. Below the banks was a cup of drier russet leaves where his friends were sprawled. This narrowed to a single tree, rather stark, with thick tufts of rough leaves resting on each bough, like wigs. It struck him as a prodigy, for it had a double trunk: the two columns almost identical in size, slightly apart, as in a colonnade.

'What's that?'

'Hm?' Hungry Rawleigh was getting his knapsack open. 'It's an alder. A black alder I think.'

'An alder ....'

'Yes. We *are* getting countrified.'

They ate and drank. After a few minutes Spurdle got out his gold-tooled guide and began to read about the Edible Dormouse (*Glis glis*). '*Bledlow Great Wood is the heart of that happy corner of England populated by dormice. The Adam and Eve of this tribe absconded from the present Lord Rothschild's celebrated menagerie at Tring Park –*'.

'What's the *date* of your book?' asked Bolswood.

'Um, let's see – 1911. I nicked it from the library at home.'

'You don't think we might miss things by following an ninety year-old guide?

'No. What? Since 1911 only horrid –'.

'Are they really edible?' A loud interruption from Rawleigh, who found Bolswood's question maddening.

'Dormice? Um .... *The Romans cherished them as a dessert, roasted, with poppy-seed and honey.* But these were farmed dormice, I gather. Reared in clay jars. Poppy-seed,' added Spurdle, settling on his back and lowering his genteel old guide over his face, 'is a by-product of opium. I used to ask for as many poppy-seed buns as I could get and grind the seeds between my teeth. But I never had visions.'

'Well if they're here, wild, oughtn't we to hunt them?'

'That seems problematic.' Spurdle's voice was sleepy, and blurred by the book. 'They hibernate for seven months or more, lucky buggers. And doubtless take immense siestas after lunch. Anyway, if you grab their tails the flesh slides off the bone. They escape.' He sighed.

'Hm. Lots of dashing about for not much meat,' observed Rawleigh, who preferred shooting game to running after it; that's what gundogs are for. Spurdle replied nothing. Bolswood was gazing at the blue vent between the two trunks of the alder. The sky gazed back from it dreadfully, like an eye through heavy lashes: a sideways eye, as if some cosmic cyclops were lying on its side. Ralph rolled over to lie on his own side, and with a thump found the heathen heaven staring straight into him.

The sun made some progress. Dapples of gold rearranged themselves on the leaves. Rawleigh was lazily at work on a pear. Their nameless meal seemed to be over. The wood had become immensely quiet. 'Do we want to go?' he yawned. 'The dormice seem to be out-napping us.'

Spurdle shut his book and sat up. 'I,' said Ralphie apologetically, still curled up, a million miles up, thousands of years back, 'am not sure I ever want to go.'

'What? From this hill? This county? This decade?'

'This particular – nook.'

'You have the soul of a dormouse. Huddle, huddle, creep back into your clay jar. Let's move. Spurdle's book says there's a good inn at Chinnor. *Crown Inn* at Chinnor, *Crown Inn* at Chinnor! If Mr Bolswood will only consent to rise.'

'I am content to lie here.'

'You are a dotard, you lack virility, you might as well be forty.' Although Rawleigh never stopped grinning, there was naked ill-feeling in his voice, as well as naked hunger. He dearly needed his leg of lamb. Bolswood managed an inane chuckle. Spurdle, stuffing his knapsack, frowned to himself, regretting, not for the first time, the excess of charity that had prompted him to invite along such a dismal specimen.

This was the hour Ralph Bolswood remembered, totting up his life quarter-of-a century later, as his happiest. Not marrying Serena, not winning *Sisk v. Van Cleef Ltd.* (against all odds, against all justice, against reason) – not taking silk, not holding his newborn son, not being knighted for certain dingy services to the Labour Party. No, the zenith of his life was walking the Icknield Way with Spurdle, who bore fools gladly, and Rawleigh, who only just tolerated him. Most of all, he remembered lying in the shallow bluebelled dip in Bledlow Great Wood, a spot where one could bed down undisturbed forever.

'Oh do come *on*, Ralphie', said Spurdle, 'stop daydreaming.'

'Sorry. Sorry.'

'And *stop*' – Rawleigh threw the core of his pear at Bolswood's forehead – 'saying "Sorry."' It bounced off his scrunched brow into a rowan thicket, and was the only dead thing the three boys left in Bledlow Great Wood, to sink into the leaf-mold and become by decay part of the hill, part of England.

ॲ

17:48. *Ka-ring ka-ring. Ka-ring ka-ring.*

ii.

We exist mainly on the inside. The mind doesn't flutter about the outside world as much as it pretends. Mostly it dozes in its cocoon of fantasy, and the pith of a man is not what he does but what he daydreams.

Ralphie grew up surrounded by normal little boys who in their daydreams swelled into a monstrous roaring giants and smashed up the world. He looked much like them, but was almost a different species. In Ralphie's fantasies the poison of self-horror was at work: he shrank. By the age of four he was flushing himself in immense loos. By eight he was dropping himself down mineshafts, firing himself into space, blowing his small limbs to shining smithereens with grenades by the blackberry hedge that backed his tree-house. At ten he liked to weigh himself down in ponds choked with waterlilies, so that bubbles of decomposition would be undetected, merely startling the frogs.

Adolescence naturally transfigured his fancies. But the new daydreams (five-act masturbatothons, with fabulous plots and chorus-lines of Nubian slavelettes) nevertheless always ended with a post-climactic scene of departure. 'Must you go?' sighed Brigitte, whom he had brutally rescued from a lesbian orgy in Act II; 'you were so masterful, so fierce'; 'I must,' and he would vanish utterly, leaving no wake in the void.

At the epoch of the Icknield Way, fornication was driving masturbation from the field. But that only let him act out post-coital oblivion in the real world. His girlfriends had to get used to a silent, almost cataleptic Ralphie; they would sigh over him a little, creep into their clothes, tiptoe away; he would not stir to watch.

The passing of time brought back childhood. Bolswood acquired a son of his own, to whom he read stories, conscientiously and tediously. Lively tones entered his voice only at such phrases as *The wolf ate him up to the last morsel* and *Nothing remained of the witch but a bad smell and a single smoking black shoe.* 'Daddy would like something to devour *him*,' reflected Tristan, sitting up in bed and trying not yawn; a piece of wisdom reached independently by judges drinking brandy in the Athenæum.

'I had Bolswood before me today.'

'My poor fellow! Was he abject?'

'He almost wept with contrition. He was simply shredding

Blagden's argument for *consensus ad idem,* and seemed to want his wig to swallow his head.'

'It's his sad little clucking noise I can't endure.'

'Yes. *That.* And the hand-wringing, such nasty spidery fingers. I had to find for him, of course.'

You will ask: 'Eh, what about being a pagan? Didn't that make a difference to this booby's inner life?' Indeed it did: it prettified the mere self-destruction of earlier fantasies. Now he hankered not merely to dissolve, but to dissolve into the cosmic womb, to mingle with the animistic spirits of flowers and stones.

However, Bolswood was always pagan in a middling or Anglican fashion. He didn't attempt theological precision. He wasn't Low Church enough to evangelise, and he wasn't High Church enough to go in for ceremonies, even such safe ceremonies as raising left fist to forehead when he first sighted the new moon. He hugged his secret heresy to himself. Its main consolation was that it was secret. No one could know his diffidence had a religious side.

Entirely private religion is necessarily a bit fey. Bolswood's faith vanished in a puff of dust when he visited Ware. His husbandhood had been (as he saw it) blotted out, and in an instant his real life, which is to say his imaginary life, shed its baroque and pious flourishes. It resolved itself into a single throbbing, obsessive image. All fancies, either of obliteration or enwombment, were wiped out – except one.

Ϙ

There were eleven days between Ralph's visit to Ware and his disappearance. During those days his inner or fantasy life became obsessive. He went about, conferred with solicitors, appeared in court and took Serena to the opera. But his waking and sleeping mind was possessed by a single scene: a helicopter's or demon-of-the-air's view of young Bolswood disappearing in, in, in, up through the pathway into the jungle that edges the mountainous Chilterns, to be cleaned away, stripped, engulfed.

There he goes, homing in on his macabre dingle. There he goes, so eagerly you might well be led to conclude (as barristers say when bullying juries) that Serena's infidelity was merely a pretext, although I think you would be mistaken in thinking so.

CŊ

Things are whipping along. We've got Bolswood humiliated, nearly stripped and buried, and I'd like to keep up momentum.

In the snow and deepening twilight beneath the double alder, Bolswood brings his final fantasy to life. He undresses, burrowing each bit of clothing where it will catch no rambler's eye – his frightful overcoat goes behind the alder itself, the cap's tossed into a mess of thorn bushes – he kicks off his shoes and pulls down his sopping trousers. A moment's pause: he hasn't brought a wallet, but there's a wad of money in the pocket – he shoves this into the crook of a bough, so those fifty-pound notes may blow away and surprise someone.

Physically his suffering is no joke. Bolswood's feet seem immersed in fire. 'Why did I ever think iciness refreshing?' When he visualised this moment he underestimated the pain. Indeed, he half-expected to die drowsily, in paradoxical warmth as the nerves failed. *Where did I read that freezing is 'a voluptuous sensation after the initial discomfort'? The man who wrote that never froze to death.* He's steadied by the liturgical seriousness of his actions. *It's the refutation of being born. I was taken out naked, wrapped in a blanket, accustomed to the light. This is debirthing.* His inner clothing, screwed into balls, is stuffed here and there. He looks round the dingle and selects a bath-sized dip in the snow. He remembers his mother. She was a keen incompetent gardener who used to gush about the charm of late snowfall. 'I'm so pleased, Ralphie! It shelters my flower-beds from the frost. Those nice little bulbs tucked up in their white blankets – aren't they cosy!' 'Oh yes mummy aren't they!' *But I was doubtful even then, she being always wrong about everything.* He kneels in his trough, and gingerly lowers himself on his hands until he is full length; then, wriggling about, he sinks.

Agony! *In extremis,* his fantasy life roars back to vigour after its eleven-day paralysis. There flash through his mind a dozen alternatives better than this. He might have crept into a crematorium after hours, fired up one of the ovens, thrust himself in. Or flown to Iceland with a fake passport to find some volcanic vent. There are warm ways into the Great Mother.

Too late, too late. He has chosen. Now he has only to push his face down into the snow (which looks, from an inch away, like ice, half-thawed by his breath, instantly hardened in the iron air). *Now. I must set my face. Make it like Zoë's. Now I push it down. This is hard. Hard as a good swimmer drowning himself.* Hard as unmaking the world. Ralph muddles light with darkness. Darkness is upon the face of the lawyer. His forehead bores into the earth, and the earth is without form and void. 'Now I must reach up, pull snow over my back and head. Now. Now.' The cold helps. Bolswood is a mammal and, if you set aside his brain, a healthy one. For half a century his body has sustained maintained its 37° against besieging air and water. Now the siege is ending in surrender. Despair of the body sets in, fiercer than any dejection of the mind. His breath is failing. His organs are preparing to shut down.

Of his mind he is losing control. This is a moment either for mental abandonment or stoic dignity, but he can't escape his usual niggling self-consciousness. He tries to frame seemly last thoughts, but what comes is childish: Zoë's heart buried behind silicone, Edible Dormice torpid in their nests, tiny bluebell bulbs interred below his stomach. *They'll be fresh this spring as when I knelt amongst them. While I, much more complicated, have no hope of coming back.*

Thinking thus Ralph Bolswood stretched forth his hand and took the coldness above his head to slay himself. His fingers reached through yielding snow to jar against something firm, leathery, furry, warm, unhibernating, swift like a hand out of heaven reaching down into his grave, a hand which scampered angrily up his own arm, groped around his jaw to find his thin unreceding hair, upon which the fingers closed, yanking his head up out of the snows so that his face was wrenched into twilight (in which the first stars were making their debut) to take a huge sobbing breath.

∾

18:21. *Ka-ring ka-ring. Ka-ring ka-ring.* Serena gives up ringing Holland Park as a bad job, sighs, and makes a fine lotus shape with her fingers to attract the bartender.

She sits enthroned on a stool. Her two crammed shopping-bags, one for lover and one for husband, perch on two stools to her right. They rest, indeed they nuzzle against each other. It's as if the *ménage à trois* she has in mind were coming into material existence.

Which it isn't. Her two men have no notion of any *ménage*. They're in horrible earnest and she is, so to speak, killing them both.

Death is sometimes the consequence of having to do with a patrician. '*Più prosecco, per favore.*' '*Certo, signora.*' A *bourgeois* bobs about in his profession as in a dinghy, a prole like Nirav floats clinging to jetsam. Serena has the air of standing on her own island, embodying the perilous charm of land just as mermaids embody the allure of the sea. (The bartender refills her glass and, unasked, puts down three more plates of tapas.) She is, of course, as estateless as anyone else. But for nine centuries her forefathers possessed their patch of the globe, their acres of Worcestershire. For four centuries, the fat times, they were little kings at Cockwood. These centuries still cling about Serena. An incomparable scent, a fine *terroir*, well-aged.

I know this sounds fulsome. But it's not just English snobbery. It affects the bartender, who is Tuscan and professional. A Tuscan's face is naturally full of life. But Angelo's face is so stern, so Aztec, that self-punishing drunks climb up to his ziggurat to have their hearts cut out. He's chiselled out of his face any sign of judgement, reserve, thought. He's tanned it like teak, or any other hard unreflecting substance. Talkative drunks can use it for hours, not finding their degradation mirrored back. You look at him and think 'Here is bartending. Makes Strong Drinks.'

Yet in his own small way Angelo remains a man. Among other things he's a fanatic of the Left and a libertine. He'd normally set about seducing such a superb foreigner as Serena, so unattached, so persistent in ringing a number that doesn't answer, so of a certain age, so sad.

But he's aware of being virtually invisible to this *donna inglese*, and this chills him. Despite her travel and her languages, Serena is parochial. Angelo stays on the periphery of her vision. He's a foreigner, which is to say a klingon, an orc, a dalek, at best a handsome curiosity like the majolica in her bag. Even back in England, Lady Bolswood has an unsettling effect on social inferiors. That's why Nirav was so accessible to her, at first. That's why her clever distinguished husband, feeling himself unwanted by her, was moved to stow himself in the soil.

iii.

'Good – evening – Sir Ralph. – Goodish. – No, baddish – in fact,'
gasped a voice in the air above him, and Bolswood felt an immense
sensation about his hips. The angel of resurrection had kicked him.
'Horrid evening. – I have – been running – uphill. – I hate running. –
I am – breathless. – I hate' (kick) 'being breathless.' This second kick
more-or-less disinterred Bolswood from his shallow ditch. He rolled
out, ending up on his back in the snow. A tall figure was bending over
him, not out of solicitude but because it appeared to be easing stitch in
its own flank. 'If I die of a heart-attack it will your fault.' A noisy breath.
'But I think I'm going to live.' A deep sighing breath. 'As are you. Get
up. And for God's sake get dressed.'

Ralph was fighting down an intolerable terror. Was he, after all,
in the Christian hell? Of the *Dea Matrona* there was certainly no sign.
Hell would explain the kicks. But the figure who had disinterred him
looked much like a mortal man, with heavy leather gloves edged with
lambswool (they had almost pulled his hair out), fur-lined overcoat and
fedora. 'And do stop gazing at me in that open-mouthed superstitious
manner. It's all right, I'm just someone you've not met before. Felix
Culpepper by name.' He pronounced the name *culper*. 'A friend of a
friend. Well, tutor of a son, which is even more respectable. Tristan
sent me to get you.'

'Tristan?' said the suicide, who could taste snow in his mouth as
Lazarus must have tasted soil. He writhed and pushed and managed to
sit up. 'Tristan doesn't know. He doesn't know what I'm doing.'

'Of course he fucking knows, you fucking imbecile,' and he was
kicked once more. 'Children know everything about their parents,
they see through them and through them, they can't help it. That's why
they're so truculent, they're *bored*. You are beginning to bore me too.
Get dressed quickly or I'll kick you to death and put you back in the
ground.'

Existence was insane. Ralph could think of nothing better to do
than obey. He started, ludicrously, to pat the ground, searching for
buried underwear.

'Tristan heard your whimpering message on his 'phone and came
round to see me. "Dr Culpepper, may I have an extension on tomorrow's

translation? The pater's topping himself this evening." "Oh?" I said. "Why?" Your trousers, cretin, are where you put them, behind that beech. He told me about you (God!), and his mother (God!), and her kept boy. "You're tremendously – "'

'*Tristan knew?*'

'Bloody hell you're thick, yes of course he knew, he's young. Can you really not remember how that works? "You're tremendously clever and practical," says Tristan, "you could stop him, I mean if you've nothing in particular to do today." Insightful boy. How did he come to be begotten by such a purblind idiot? He'll get a good Second if not disturbed by family suicides. "You may not have an extension," I told him. "I forbid your father's death. Go to the lodge and get me a cab. I expect you here tomorrow at ten with your Horace finished." He promised. I caught the 8:55 to King's Cross. On the way I rang your house, and spoke to your colourful housekeeper, who confirmed your intention –'.

'I –'

'"I didn't mention to my Polack housekeeper that I was killing myself" – God. Really I wonder if it's proper to allow stupidity like yours to stay above ground.' Culpepper cocked his head to watch the gormless fellow button his shirt. The snow was so crisp it had frosted rather than soaked Bolswood's clothes. 'I rang your chambers and found you'd gone in to work. Exactly the spiritless gesture I'd expect from you on the day of your death. So I had a few hours. I did what you should have done. I went to Dagenham and looked up Nirav Ghosh.'

Bolswood, who had one sock on and was bewilderedly pawing bushes for the other, made the apologetic noise in his palate.

'He was lounging about his uncle's dry-cleaning business off Globe Road. "I am a friend of your belovèd," I cried. "I have great news. Her evil husband is frequenting a fancy woman. Let us track him and catch him in the act. Your belovèd will leave him in abhorrence and marry you. My taxi's waiting." All of which Ghosh swallowed. The cretin. Serena seems to have a *penchant* for the dimmest men. Is it a sexual kink?' Bolswood's legs were in the air, contending with semi-solid icy trousers. 'Although it's only fair to reflect how many Bollywood films Ghosh must have seen. Films with clunky romantic plots much like the story I spun for him. He has that excuse. I can't imagine what your excuse is.' The noise again. 'Tristan has complained to me about that aural *tic* of yours. "The daddy-noise." Stop it.' Ralph did stop, and will not do it again till his dying day. 'Well, Ghosh leapt into the cab with me. We drove back to the Temple, and spent a dull two hours staking out your chambers. Well, dull for me. He eagerly unburdened his so-called heart to me. Poor homunculus. I was groaning with tedium by the time you emerged. In a cheap overcoat which is behind that alder. And an infernal baseball cap. Which is behind that bush. No, don't put it on again, give it to me,' and Culpepper chucked it deep into the thickening darkness. 'The coat we'll have to put up with. Shoes over there, and there. We followed your 'bus to Marylebone, pursued you onto the train, changed carriage when you did. It was easy to follow you. Do you realise how conspicuous you looked, lurking your way across the Home Counties in your child's hat?'

Random nonsense was pressing on Bolswood from within his brain, just as nonsense crushed him from without. It seemed best to stand out of the way. So he said: 'But everyone wears them.'

'Your thoughts are confused. No, half-baked. They don't go on long enough to become confused. Can't you see that it's one thing for everyone to do something, and an entirely different thing for a person to do it because everyone does it? It feels different. It looks different. Do it because you do it and you're invisible. Do it to be seen doing it and you're like a mime artist performing on the street, with clown make-up and a hat laid out for coins. No of course you can't grasp this. Don't hurt your head trying, just find your socks. I suppose a barrister's bound to be bad at hiding himself. Your livelihood's lying by exaggeration. You've no concept of deceit through reticence.'

Bolswood would normally have a retort to hand. But he answered nothing, for the curious reason that he'd been suddenly winded. His physical pain was receding, but his mind was rolling over and over, as if tumbled in surf. How beautiful this grove was, ever blasted by winter. He was so astonished by its beauty that he couldn't speak. It seemed to him that as the last light of day leaked away, the dimensions of the whole universe were shifting. There was subdued brightness of snow; then silhouettes of trees; then, beyond, dark glory illimitable. Glory crashed over him. How could he not have noticed it before? The splendour!

'We got out at Saunderton and popped into the waiting room, hanging back to let you get going. Not that it mattered. You couldn't hear us, stomping along with your head down. I was sure by now what you were about. You meant to vanish. So we didn't have to worry about gunshots. Or sudden leaps under passing lorries. You were bound for the depths of the woods. We simply had to trail you.' Bolswood was pushing his feet, one in a frosty sock and one bare, into his snowy shoes.

'My idea, of course, was to have you confront your rival. To set up a place of resolution. If you met Nirav deep in lonely woods all the better. But I'd made a mistake. I'd forgotten what my grandpapa Osbert used to say: "Awful fellas, Bengalis, they run under heavy mortar fire." Grandpapa was an Anglo-Indian of the old school. Nirav is a Bengali, sure to be soft. It was foolish of me to assume he could walk. He started wailing about cold the instant we left the station. He got slower and slower. It's been very aggravating. You soon passed out of sight. Fifteen minutes ago I realised I was going to be too late, which would have irritated me beyond bearing. Not too late because you'd be dead. No one suffocates in snow as powdery as this, and it takes hours to freeze past hope of resuscitation. Too late because you'd already have gone to earth and become, in this failing light, invisible. You follow? So I left him and ran. Which hurt me. Damn you. I was just in time to see your fat bottom wallowing under the snow.'

'Nirav is *here*?' cried Bolswood, for whom existence had settled into a pattern of widening madness. His gloves were on; except for his head he was fully clothed. Perhaps if he did what this thin self-important fellow said, and didn't try to think, he'd blunder out of chaos and start understanding things again.

'Yes. Mr Ghosh is waiting at the bottom of this hill. I left him shivering with apprehension in the lee of a copse. I promised to rescue him shortly. But I think it's you that should do the rescuing.'

'You want me to go down and talk to him?'

'Talk to him? *Talk* to him? What, put on your wig and make your case from common law? Explain that you'd prefer him not to sleep with your wife? Good heavens, man, do you think the universe is woven of competitive argument? In the beginning was the Quibble? God. Listen. Listen imaginatively.' He looked round, found a likely branch, positioned his gloved hands on it, and pulled as hard as he could. It bent. 'I'm going to speak elliptically,' observed Culpepper, working his branch back and forth. Tiny globules of ice came loose from the branch and littered the drifts. 'The thing about adultery is that the bodies all look the same. If you swapped the faces over, it wouldn't *look* wrong.' Again he strained at the wood. It cracked but wouldn't loosen. 'Your mistake, I think, was muddling the faces in your mind. It's just – to make a childish indecency – a question of the wrong fellow in the right hole.' And he let his eyes rest for a moment on the dimple in the snow. It still bore the print of Ralph's body. Ralph could make out the heavy outline of his chest and head, the deep indentation of belly, the blur of hapless little feet.

For a long half-minute Ralph regarded his burial-place. It looked distressingly like the snow-angels children make (even miseries of children, like young Ralphie) by lying in fresh snow and waggling their arms and legs. He felt no guilt at having made the shape and being there in the earth. He felt no guilt for having left, and being here on top of the earth. He was reborn beyond apology. So he broke off his another branch, smaller than Culpepper's because he wasn't as strong. He turned, and stomped off along the track that descends Wain Hill.

ை

'My round. Seb?'

'More Guinness.'

'Tristan? *Tristan?*'

'Sorry. Sorry. Miles away. Bitter, please. A half.'

'Hmph.' Ollie went up to the bar.

Seb eyed his friend. 'Well?'

'Family. Bloody bores.'

'They always are. I've got a French aunt who sends me twenty-page letters without a cheque attached.'

'*My* aunt lives in Ware and tries to borrow money from *me*.'

'You win that one. Fuck.'

'Anyway this is worse still. Y' know my undead mother's shagging this thing from Tower Hamlets?'

'Yah, I remember.'

'Well, the pater's found out and wants to do himself in. I had a call from him this morning.'

'That's silly,' said sensible Ollie, coming back from the bar with a pint in each hand. 'I didn't get you a half. That's silly too. I think the Bolswoods must be a silly family.'

'I think we are.' Ollie went back for Guinness. 'Anyway I told Culpepper and he's gone up to London to stop him.'

'What's the problem, then? Culpepper's infallible.'

'Yes I know. *But what about work?* I can't bunk off anything now.

Not once he's saved my father's life. Every time he sets me an essay I'll have to do it.'

'True. That's bad. Ah!' Ollie had reappeared and gave Seb his stout. 'No doubt that's why he's doing it. Cruel bastard, Culpepper. Cheers.'

☙

Over the last two months Nirav had approached the threshold of humanity. Beneath that scant hair, held flat to the skull by Stud's *Vigueur Humide*, prodigious ideas had crackled, like lightning in a cistern. Behind those piggy cheeks and cattle eyes an improbable emotion had reared up, and broken him to bits, like a volcano pushing up through a parking-lot. Tufts of grass peeked amidst the scorched, sterile rubble. Nirav was not yet a person, but the materials of personhood were beginning to show.

I suspect these tufts would all have died away had his affair with Serena gone on any longer. But there's no way of being sure, and the fact is he did make himself a victim with his infatuation. He shed his blood for love, he courted martyrdom. Nirav stands enrolled with Mark Antony, Romeo Montague and Francesco di Rimini.

The husband is approaching, baleful and cudgel-wielding, crunching down a snowy hillside in Buckinghamshire. It's not for you or me to sneer at the lover. I think we might honour these last minutes before Bolswood arrives by visiting the inside of Nirav's head.

We are immediately shocked. What are these fur-lined white Mercedes, girls in bikinis and pearl necklaces, simpering capering butlers toting magnums of champagne? What is this Lear jet painted cursively *Bennykins & Belle* in gilt along its fuselage? Alas, this is how the poor chump pictures his mistress' life. He's a child of the twenty-first century, with a fundamentalist faith in garish magazines and pulp videos. He takes these puerile fantasias as somber reports of the world to come, the world as it should be. This is the world from which he hopes to rescue Belle; it is also the world, in a confused way, he hopes to share with her.

So much for the uppermost level of Nirav's brain. Beneath comes a lukewarm stratum, pinky-gray and slowly bubbling, like a seam of liquid soap. This is love as such: the passion of love as it exists within Nirav Ghosh. The surprise here is not how childish he is, but how babyish. The odd pornographic or sensual figure goes swirling through the slime. But the texture of his affection is much as when it was centred on Mrs Ghosh's breast. Even the words that bubble in the pinkness are milk-fed infant words: 'Nirav *want*', 'Nice, nice', 'Nirav like Belle', 'Nirav like Belle b'wee much', 'Belle like Nirav?', 'Soft, warm', 'Tuddle'.

Sink still further into Nirav's mind and I'm sorry to say we hit self-pity, which is his bedrock. It's not very pretty. Nirav lead a soft life in Dagenham. He has always been idle, he has always coddled himself, he has never been cold before. He was moved from the urban Midlands to London as a ten year-old, and has scarcely set foot in the countryside since. As far as possible, he's never even outside. Today's journey has filled him, once the excitement oozed away, with dismay. It's not that he's morally alarmed by John (which is how Felix cautiously introduced himself), nor that he dreads meeting Bennykins (as he calls Bolswood). The snowy copses and fields, in the failing light, simply frighten him. 'God, it's awful leaving the station. God, what a spooky wood. God, it hurts walking along beside John. Actually, trotting. Jogging, actually.' Nirav never exercises, and the pains in thigh and lung are novel and distressing. He is quite frankly scared of the dark.

These are the trifling weaknesses of a child, which a few days of normal life might dispel. But it seems that it time is done with Nirav Ghosh. He is not to have those few days. He can hear stomping coming back down the hill. Nirav looks up a little weepily, to welcome John and beg to be taken home. But it is not John: it's a man he has never seen before, obviously a lunatic. Perhaps all wild woods contain naughty lunatics! This one is wet through his suit and overcoat, bare-headed, ice-haired, wild-faced, flushed, bruised, and brandishing a thingy – one of those wooden sticking-out-things you get on the side of trees, not trees with their leaves off but the ones that still have spiky what's-its on them, like Christmas trees only, y'know, made with dark green needly what's-its not silver tinsel, and no lights.

ಚಿ

Now you are to imagine Culpepper standing alone in the darkening snowy wood, smoking a black cigarette of Turkish sun-cured tobacco made by Fribourg & Treyer and monogrammed *F.C.*

Culpepper smoked and stared at the darkening sky. The moon, huge and one day shy of being full, was lifting herself above the Chilterns. He watched the glow of his ash become fiercer as the world faded around it. And he listened to the sounds from below: shriek, thud, whimper, thud, thud; then the noise of harsh exhalation and slow progress.

Ralph came into view. He was fit enough, what with his squash and skiing and riding. But it's no small thing to carry a chubby man up a slope through heavy snow. Ralph's face was mottled, each breath scraped his lungs.

Nirav's face lolled across Ralph's shoulder. There was a spectacular mess of black above the left eye. Felix watched and did not offer to help. Ralph worked his way over the roots and dips in the snow and finally reached the shallow he had chosen for himself an hour before. Into this he heaved Nirav, face down. The fall of the body made a dull swish. Ralph stood with his right hand clutching his chest, and might have stayed standing there for a while, had Felix not produced a small electric torch from his overcoat pocket, handed it over with the sketch of a bow – 'Keep it out of my eyes' – then he turned his back to face the triumphant sphere of the moon.

Stiff as an old man, Ralph knelt. He worked off his rival's shoes, pitiful white trainers, trousers, puffy jacket, hooded sweatshirt. He thrust this clothing into a thorn bush, beneath a fallen trunk, within a rotten bole, under drifts of snow, out of sight. Once he got off the shirt and undershirt (Mrs Ghosh insisted on undershirts), he could see Nirav's bare back moving slightly up and down. His body looked poignant, as bodies always do from behind. Bolswood might have felt compunction, except that he caught a trace of Urban HitMan. This was the smell which began the trouble. His bland face set into bitter lines. What he thought was: *Welcome to my cold bed, small enemy.* What he said was: 'It's finished.'

Felix answered without turning. 'You're entirely free of this, Bolswood. The carcase will never be found. But if it is, nothing connects it to you. And if anything does, still absolutely nothing connects it with me. I don't know how the law of evidence works. But I hope – if you ever talk in your sleep, or get religion, or make some ghastly mistake; if you end up being questioned by the police – you will remember. My name will not come up. And if it does come up: I did not suggest this.'

'No,' said Ralph, who was making sure none of Nirav's clothing showed anywhere.

'I did not hand you the stick.'

'No.' Ralph began covering Nirav, kicking over him his cosy white blanket.

'I did not even see you do it.'

The boy was gone. 'Yes. Can we go?'

'You chose a good spot,' remarked Felix, turning round and casting his eye pleasantly over the clearing, as if at the end of a successful picnic. Full night was upon them. Moonlight turned everything to pewter or black paper. 'Give me back the torch.' He flashed it about. 'Well away from paths. A basin deep enough to remain out of sight before full leafage. Sheltered by that dense line of shrub. And it's a damp clearing, to judge by the sag of that bank and that misshapen alder. There must be a spring nearby. Clothes will molder the sooner. Foxes will find him as soon as it thaws, crows will polish off the bits; then it'll be time for frolicsome earthworms. You look awful. Can you walk? Well then, walk. In front of me, please. Lead the way. I'll manage the light.'

CHAPTER 3
Epoch of the Moon

i.

The walk down Wain Hill should form the end of this story, especially for Sir Ralph Bolswood, to whom, however, it came to seem the beginning of all things. For the rest of his long and curiously cheerful life he remembered it as something absolutely apart.

This didn't have to do with the foolish hours of self-harm that preceded it. Nor did it have to do with the day that followed, which he spent comfortably cycling through hot bath, whisky, bed, again and again – once visiting his new friend in hospital, where the doctors said he was out of danger – until he, Bolswood, was ready for the airport and Florence.

The descent through Bledlow Great Wood was as cleanly cut off from the rest of his life as an opera. An overture ends; lights come up on a stage-set; things occur; it's a masterpiece; the lights go down and you go away, into different surroundings, changed.

There were various reasons for this cut-offedness. To begin with, he was in a physical state he'd never known before, being at once battered and refreshed. It's good for anyone, certainly any lawyer, to be kicked about. His clothes had set into armour. He walked creaking over the snow in a suit of ice. His emotions, too, seemed safely walled away from him. He felt for Culpepper the rapturous dread the newborn must feel for the midwife; a general terror and even more terrible joy lay all beyond. None of it could not touch him.

In years to come, Ralph Bolswood never ceased to meditate on that downward stroll. And this is what he'd think: 'It wasn't really like grand opera. It was more solemn. No dialogue, no plot. No commentary. I didn't say a word. I thought of things to say but kept silence. Not very barrister-like. It was a showing. It was immense. Even Culpepper's relentless patter couldn't spoil it. I suppose great ceremony foresees and incorporates interruption. Heckling's folded into the rite. And this was a rite. Like the Mysteries perhaps. How flustered the initiate must have been, coming out from the city to Eleusis! The night-long vigil. A night of darkness, of sudden noise. Chanting by white-robed hierophants, blindfoldings and unblindfoldings. He's led from pitch-black cell to cell, hears verses whispered from hidden galleries, cries, sudden gongs. A knife rests on his throat, blood's poured over him, blood's washed away. At last, at dawn, he's unbound and shown an ear of wheat. The blazon of the universe. Explanation. The edge of truth has been worked loose, so it can peel away for the rest of his life. It was like that, coming down Wain Hill. Nothing happened. But it was the most important thing that ever happened to me.'

ଔ

On they went down the hill.

Culpepper was a don, a superior type. Dons are addicted to airing their sham-omniscience. They're used to the adulation or mock-adulation of impressionable youths. Even ironic praise slakes their desperate thirst. It's hard for such men not to chatter. After an inner struggle lasting ten minutes, Culpepper flung aside his dignity.

'You're very silent, Bolswood. I hope you're not brooding. Speaking for myself, *je ne regrette rien*. I relish the concept of burial alive. Although I prefer other people to do it. I mean the burying as well as the being buried. It's classically sparse. No method could have cleaner lines (except simply holding your breath forever, which I don't think can be done). Self-burial! No violence but the innate violence of weather, no weapon but the earth itself. I wonder, how many other people were secretly interred tonight? You know that a quarter of a million Englishmen drop from sight every year? Seven hundred a day. I like numbers; I'm going speak in numbers for a bit. About half of those reported missing turn up sooner or later. Of the rest, let's say two-thirds are successful runaways (and who's to blame them? The families you see on 'buses, on the street). That leaves thirty thousand who are dead. Mainly suicides, but at the very least ten thousand must be murderees. Every couple of days someone trips over a stiff and the razzas have no idea which of the ten thousand it is. They fossick about with its teeth and D.N.A., but generally it maintains the anonymous pathos of roadkill. The authorities don't bring these statistics to our attention, fearing that we'll grasp how safe it is to do someone in. Or do yourself in and never be found, which calls for much the same technique – as you've been demonstrating. We're fed detective fiction to make us think murder is rare, and requires fiendish cunning, and is nonetheless always solved. Mere propaganda. To cause someone to vanish requires no more than normal intelligence, the sort necessary to drive a car, the sort you possess. Murderers only get caught if they want to get caught: everyone knows that. Despite the anxiety of our masters, we're all secretly aware how easy it is to kill. And that fact enchants me. It proves that humanity is doused with love, I mean universal love, the interesting sort: love of the enemy. We're all balanced on a cliff, anyone can nudge anyone off, and everyone has scores of enemies. If aggrieved husbands or bored wives or resentful colleagues habitually did what they know they can do, there'd be carnage. But that doesn't happen. It doesn't even happen in America, where everyone goes about armed like a Congolese mercenary. And in England, instead of general slaughter we have this perfectly reasonable rate of ten thousand unsolved murders *per annum*. Which is probably the minimum necessary for the nation's spiritual health. I say this to put Master Ghosh in context.'

Nirav! thought Bolswood, in a dazed fashion. *Universal love!*

CƷ

It would be saccharine to say he loved Nirav. Nonetheless, his imagination did dance at the thought of Nirav Ghosh's existence. He could even see at a distance the mountain of cinders which would be repenting of his death; and like a master mountaineer, he was sure he would reach that peak in the end. You'll say that it was impertinent of him to imagine feeling remorse for Ghosh when Ghosh wasn't yet dead. And so it was. Bolswood's brain was churning, and producing bizarre thoughts which did not seem random. It churned not because of what had just happened, nor because of Culpepper's prattle, but because of what he was seeing. On the way up Bledlow Great Wood had seemed simply a waste, a forest under snow at night, the most desolate England gets. But now the complexity of the bare beeches moved him as he didn't know he could be moved. The shapes were extravagant because they were so free: the trunks seemed to have no need to push upward, they struck postures as in a dance. Gravity was nothing: silver arabesques hung, leapt, floated in mere darkness. On one side the boughs were perfect silver: the other side was perfect black, invisible, swallowed by night. Almost the effect was stagey, for wherever he looked the trees opened and framed a white stage, which had no sharp background, but ran off beyond geometry and dimension into pure blankness. Not white, pearl; he thought of black-and-white photographs made on gelatin silver paper; but it seemed obscene to say 'monochrome' when he could count, what, a dozen shades against the inky silhouette. He was lost in rapture. It was past belief how wonderful they were. And the snow! Snow did not look like the background, in seemed painted on, positive and bright: oblongs of it between the trunks were up-thrusting fingers, gesturing: snow was a hierophant. And the beeches were the alphabet of the language of creation. As every great painter must first be a great draughtsman, so these fantastic skeleton shapes were the material for designing all vegetation, all complexity of living form, the glories of amoeba, bluebells, alders, dormice, Serena. Nirav. Even – and this was the great leap – of Ralph Ackerley Bolswood. The light of Culpepper's torch jumbled with his legs as he walked so that beams of light and dark thrust forward and danced their way into the forest's stripes of black and white, and for the first time in his life he felt himself a creature among creatures.

℃

And still Felix babbled away.

'Master Ghosh, Master Ghosh! I don't suppose anyone will consider our little friend again. Let the human mind offer him a last farewell. "I wish you joy of the worm."' Culpepper turned rococo. 'Nirav's thoughts are prorogued; they'll be dissolved before they can re-assemble; his Hansard will have nothing more to record.' Culpepper sighed. 'Not that they amounted to much. But it's sobering to remember that he was, like us, a product of tertiary education. He told me about it. Two modules nearly complete at Creekmouth Community College. Do we see the lecturer in media studies from Creekmouth Community College stomping up this hill to drag thingy from his grave? No. Which shows that the ancient universities have a point, even for ineducable hobbledehoys like your son.' A sneer at Tristan would normally have roused Bolswood. But his eyes had lifted themselves from the trees to the starry, moony, half-clouded sky, and his mind had reached a new pitch of exultation, which Culpepper, insinuating as a temptor, could not sully. 'All of me is on the outside,' thought Bolswood. 'Even my thoughts fall on me from outside, like starlight on a rock. I'm like one of those pinpricks up there, a chink by which majesty too great to be borne works its way into the finite world. Sit still, the universe washes over you, layer by layer. The layer of sense, the layer of pain and pleasure, and beneath – well, what can words do with it? Swiftness, complexity too bright and fierce to be called joy, but perhaps joy is its shadow. – The beeches!'

This sort of thinking has a bad press, which it deserves. But in Bolswood's case rhapsody justified itself with heightened perception. For instance, the small part of his mind that was attending to Culpepper's chatter perceived what most of Culpepper's friends never have. Feline self-satisfaction, or satanic neatness, which most people think forms Felix's essence, is armour that he buckles on. Beneath was somthing weak and soft, but human. Bolswood understood Culpepper in the fixed and certain way a child understands, and for the same reason, which is humility.

Humility is irreparable, it stains the mind. The half hour he spent coming down through Bledlow Great Wood ruined Bolswood as a barrister. He was no longer fit to lead out packs of lies against other packs of lies. He could never argue another case.

'More about me,' said Culpepper, after a few minutes of trying to keep quiet. 'Why am I such a melancholy grave-robber? Oughtn't I to be in a triumphant mood? Shouldn't I be congratulating myself on aborting a human sacrifice? Replacing the human with a ram, or rather a podgy lambkin? The problem is that the lamb was also human. Well, at least as human as you. Difficult, difficult. I blame Lady Bolswood. She's tangled things up so thoroughly only death could untangle. It had to be you or that wretched Bengali. I can't see there's not much odds, you're both detritus. But the fact is you have a son at my college and Nirav doesn't. Wygyfortis is the stupidest college in Cambridge and Tristan is our least stupid classicist. He may scrape a Second, which makes him important scum. I couldn't let him get distracted by a family suicide and go down with a Pass degree. So here we are, and I hope you will always treat Tristan with subdued gratitude. I mean, here's the bridleway.' They had come to the bottom of the hill. The path ran left and right before them. 'No, this way, Bolswood, not back toward Saunderton. (You know the suffragettes burned down the

station exactly a hundred years ago next week? Creepy coincidence.)
Chinnor's closer, and from Chinnor I can get a taxi straight back to
Cambridge. I have, by the way, the money you left in that tree. Some
for you' – he unpeeled a little of a wet wad of paper – 'the rest is for my
cab. It's our annual pancake supper at ten, and I want to be there. An
old Combination Room tradition. You remember it's Shrove Tuesday
I hope? Bear it in mind. Perhaps we could think of recent events as
carnival. None of us has been on best behaviour, but perhaps we needed
to get rambunctiousness out of our systems. And we're masked, so to
speak. The consequences of ours frolics are muted. By the way, I'll drop
by Tristan's rooms and let him know you're all right. He'll be up. His
Horace is due tomorrow morning, which means an all-nighter. He's
been indolent, but after all it's only Lent Term which gives us time.
He's promised to work from now on, being under an obligation.' The
first house. The track was turning into a village street. 'The Icknield
Way! What a track! Aren't you moved by it? Even before Cæsar and his
charning legions showed up, this road led out of shamanistic murk to
the coast, the open sea, Rome, the luminous Empire, the wide rational
world. And, of course, *vice versa.* "The pater's religiously neolithic,"
Tristan told me this morning; "elves and totems, you know, and being
slurped up by Mother Earth when he dies." I trust you're over that
backwardness now. Millions of people over thousands of years have
scuttled up and down this road as fate ordained. The important thing's
to go in the right direction. All roads lead anywhere. In your case, I
think, this road leads out of Bledlow Great Wood and into Italy.' They
were emerging from the trees now. They could see the pub, gaudy
and jolly, at the end of the dim little street. 'I heard Nirav's account of
himself: he amounted to about a third of a man, although perhaps he
was growing bigger. You're a frozen puddle, Lady Bolswood's a puff of
steam. You have between you about enough material for quarter of a
human being. I suggest you form that demi-semi-person – what else
can you do? Go home. Remember you've given Łucja four days off:
you'll have to fix your own supper. Recover. Fly out to Florence. Win
back your wife. She'll be a receptive mood. Anyway you have an unfair
advantage over your rival: he's vanished. As she'll discover when she
gets home. Persuade her that he must have got frightened, fled, is back,
say, with relations in India. She'll be troubled for a few weeks, but if
you are being a loving husband she'll want to believe you. He'll drop
from sight. And Bolswood: give her more children. She's surely still

nubile. Tristan's particular strain of idiocy is sentimental, I think he'd be amused to acquire a sibling at this late date. Well, at least a baby sister, someone who's not going to reduce his inheritance too much. She'll introduce a certain freshness and gaiety, begotten by tomb-bait carrion though she be – I may say that to a Master of the Bench of the Middle Temple. All's well that ends well, eh? If you hadn't tried contaminating the soil of Buckinghamshire with your person, I wouldn't have been summoned, nor would you now be free of your rival. Thus it's despair and burial that have brought you to this' – Culpepper, the showman, had been padding his remarks so they come to a halt before *The Crown* just as he pronounced – 'happy ending.'

The pub signboard, Bolswood noticed, was new, not the one that hung when he was last here, eating roast lamb with Spurdle and Rawleigh. Strange he should remember the old one so well. Everything was strange. (He was now possibly light-headed, what with cold and exhaustion.) Dimly he heard Culpepper clucking with irritation. The tidy ending, he gathered, was slightly disarranged: there was only one taxi outside *The Crown*. The single cabman was eyeing them dubiously in the gloom, although the gloom was lightening. There was a peculiar light crowning Wain Hill. The cloud was thinning.

'Goodish evening. No, good evening. Can you take me all the way to Cambridge? Excellent. And is there another cab you can ring for my, my, well my friend? No? *No?* Hm. Well, Bolswood,' with disgust, 'I suppose I'll have to give you a lift as far as Princes Risborough, where you can get a train to King's Cross. You will try not get the seat too wet as you thaw, won't you, Bolswood? Bolswood? Bolswood? What are you doing? Bolswood?'

But Ralph only stared and stared up, above the summit of Bledlow Great Wood. The silver radiance tangled in the clouds had freed itself. The moon had lifted her face from the snowy hills.

ii.

Gentle reader, or rather, m'Lud: the only excuse for what follows is that the moon is a quirk. Unlike the sun and earth, she needn't exist. We would have evolved without her. Indeed the young earth was moonless and got by perfectly well. Then for no particular reason it was struck by a smaller planet – in billiards I believe this is called a two-ball cannon. The smaller planet blew up, the earth's mantle burst into space and for a few weeks things were in unimaginable disorder. When the debris coalesced, a gratuitous silver circle was sailing through the night sky, waxing and waning mysteriously. Or not sailing, *whizzing*. To begin with the moon crossed the sky thrice a day and looked a dozen times the size she is now. There can't have been much night-sky left to speak of. This calamity occurred four-and-a-half billion years ago, and –

THE READER, PRESIDING: Mr Author, I confess that what you say bewilders me. You story, as I understand, covers a few hours of 5th March 2014, with a number of tiresome flashbacks. Is that right? I'm not clear where this prehistorical evidence is taking us.

AUTHOR: M'Lud, the case for the defence is that Sir Ralph is about to escape our narrative, escape the entire novel form, into a state of grace. I wish to demonstrate why that is possible. I crave your Lordship's patience.

Since her spectacular days of infancy, the moon has receded to her present distance, slowed down, and given herself the airs of a fixture. But earth remains aghast at the calamity, and somehow our planet's attitude seeps into our minds.

Of necessity the sun moves and burns and decays. All other physical basics of existence – weight, sky, procreation, night-time, age, colour, ingestion, death – seem self-evident too; it's affectation to pretend they surprise us. But the moon remains disconcerting. The test is that we can imagine doing without her. It's easy to picture another ball coming along to pot her into the solar flames, or knock her into baulk beyond the asteroid belt. Four-and-a-half billion year haven't dulled the caprice. It seems fantastic to us that night should sometimes be hoarily lit up. The moon's startling as a comet.

She proves the liberty of events. What the moon shines on is often as giddy as herself. What is lunar is vagarious, arbitrary and gratuitous, and there's more of it in human affairs than policemen and psychologists divulge. Daily or at least nightly life is full of wilder happenings than we can imagine or explain. That is one reason prose fiction is so feeble, and the fable comparatively satisfying. Life will not always abide the proprieties of the adult novel. The novel is too earnest to be quite serious. A novelist is a zealot for psychological contingency. He dangles his characters before us like pirates gibbetted in chains at Wapping Stairs, grimly bound in causal necessity –

THE LITERARY CRITIC OF *THE LONDON REVIEW OF BOOKS*, PROSECUTING: Objection, M'Lud. Surely we could be spared this harangue against the very tenets of novel-writing? We have to consider the feelings of any literary persons who might be listening.

THE READER, PRESIDING: I must say I agree. Mr Author, might we return to the doings or misdoings of Sir Ralph Bolswood? I urge you to indulge fewer allusions.

AUTHOR: I am most profoundly grateful to your Lordship for your guidance.

To recapitulate: the moon, that *arriviste* and freak, shone shyly into the upturned face of Ralph, an immortal soul destined, we are told, from before time to live after time is done. And he was even more wanton than herself. The moon is a permanent wound of miracle, a rend in the fabric of cause and effect: a voiding of the law: an outrage against regularity: proof that there's nothing to stop a planet spinning out of nowhere to collide. Bolswood swerved for no good reason, or rather for no reason I can point to inherent in what has gone before. A planet struck, against which there is no law. No tale can explain why a man is what he is, except to say he is what he finally does: and nothing can explain *that*. Fiction merely brings us closer to the brink of human liberty, a chasm so deep our eyes cannot reach the bottom.

THE READER: Ahem.

AUTHOR: This is what Bolswood did in the car park of *The Crown* in Chinnor: he turned to Felix and lifted his, Felix's, arms into the air

(Felix was too amazed to resist), patted his (Felix's) overcoat until he found the electric torch, removed it, made a mock bow, spun on his heel, marched off into the woods, and for the third time in his life began the ascent of Wain Hill.

LONDON REVIEW OF BOOKS: M'Lud! I am sorry, but this gets worse and worse. My learned friend is purporting to tell us *a story*. Of a purportedly comic sort. If what I gather is about to happen is indeed about to happen, the joke comes undone. To exhume one character may be regarded as a misfortune; to exhume two looks like carelessness.

THE READER: Oh, ho, yes. Most amusing. Apt.

LONDON REVIEW OF BOOKS: The work of the previous chapter is about to be carelessly unravelled. Dr Culpepper went to some trouble, and employed credible ingenuity, rescuing Sir Ralph from his grave, and disposing of Mr Ghosh in that same untenanted locale. Lady Bolswood's disreputable affair is vitiated; her sexual future is, I take it, assured. When matters have been tidied up in a satisfactory manner, what possible sense can there be in untidying them again? Such clumsy backtracking spoils the plot. I submit that it wrecks whatever point it has. M'Lud, I move that this story be thrown out.

THE READER: Mr Author?

AUTHOR: This is undeniably a wayward turn, m'Lud. But our case is that what occurs beneath the moon doesn't have to be responsible to narrative sense. It is merely *so*. The world is too gratuitous for well-knit plots. It goes by prank.

Here, for instance, is another capricious development. Culpepper stood watching Bolswood until he disappeared into the weird lunar light and dark of the wood. But then, once he had passed out of earshot, Culpepper whooped, slapped his thigh, threw back his head to guffaw at the heavens, and was still suffering unexplained triumphant laughter when he got into his cab, so that the cabbie, who had been rejoicing over his fat fare, began to think it will be a long hundred minutes to Cambridge.

In due course Culpepper quieted down, and by turns dozed or sang opera (to the deepening dismay of the cabbie), and considered how much of the evening's elegant, abortive thuggery he should reveal to Tristan.

More wasted effort, more vanity. Despite his promise, Tristan had already bunked his translation and gone off with Seb to the Girton party.

This doesn't surprise you, Lord Reader, does it? You looked for nothing better from young Bolswood, and for some pages you've had your eye on the depraved females of Girton. One of whom, by the way, is listening open-mouthed as Tristan plays the suicide card. 'Yar, well I *am* atch rally rally sad because my daddy's threatening to – to – well, to do himself harm'; he even manages a catch in his voice. She's the third girl on whom he's tried this little speech. Daring tactics, since there are only thirty girls at the party, and sooner or later they'll start comparing notes. Numbers One and Two sniggered, but Tristan deemed the ploy worth one more bash, and behold! in Number Three he has found the college *ingénue*. Who says: 'That's rally *soooo* terrible. Let's score some more of these scrumptious pancakes and go back to my rahm. You can tell me *all* about it', then steers him to the door. Tristan presses a knuckle to his mouth, as if to suppress a manly sob, but the other hand, the left, the hand of curse, exchanges congratulatory slaps with Seb on the way out into the moonlit quad.

Enough of this young scoundrel. Enough of the whole pack of them! It is twenty-six past eight Greenwich Mean Time. Time to ring down the curtain on our farce.

iii.

It's not the custom for characters to take a bow (and perhaps find themselves hissed). We're going to line them up nonetheless, taking one last disgusted gaze at each. They don't warrant much attention, because by and large they're perpetrating predictable behaviour.

First the lowlife.

At this moment, that is, 20:26 on the fourth of March 2014, Angela Flank is gossiping about the Bolswoods to her indifferent boyfriend. 'Well anyway I thought Lady B. sounded ever so suspicious. "Where is he?" she hissed. I smell messy divorce big time. And what's *she* doing in the Med then? You remember what Ibiza was like, Kev. Kev? … Bugger me blind with a marrow, he's asleep again.'

Łucja, better-informed but just as boring, retails the lamentable misdeeds of her infidel *Anglicy* to her hard-bitten Slough-dwelling sister, whom nothing can shock, and who waits, scarcely-listening, for her turn to take up the lament on everyone, everything, everywhere, like a low sustaining drone on a bagpipe. The sisters took up this drone from their mother before them, in some hamlet of the Pipet Marshes; they've picked out the meagre notes of their lives above it; it has grounded, it has steadied them; they mean to pass it on to their daughters.

Raspberry cream liqueur is Felicity and Clod's tipple tonight. This evening, as every evening, they've slapped and harried Rat, Brat, Fat and long-eared Bat into bed. Now they can get down to business. Eight twenty-six: happy epoch. Sweet ladies, how cruelly are you tethered to the sun! It comes up, your heads hurt; it reaches its zenith, your sufferings ebb; it goes down into the sea, your thirst submerges you; it reaches the longitude of Hawaii, you pass out. Good-night then, ladies, good-night. Good-night Mog. 'Sss.' Our last glimpse is lit like nightmare, for they're switched off the overhead and left on their green-glowing cellphones, the better to enjoy the glugging of pink spirit into a pitcher of liquid nitrogen. This is stage one of making a frothy smoking cocktail called Beckham's Penis. You shan't have the full recipe from me. Wool of bat and tongue of dog, for all I know; finger of birth-strangled babe ditch-delivered by a drab.

'But a Penis would have been perfect,' whispers Fat to her sister and brothers lying in the dark, as they do, crowded onto a brocaded chesterfield and a Regency day-bed. Brat, the baby, wriggles with pleasure: 'All dat cweam. They'd never taste it not 'til too late when they thtart kweaming.' Rat's unconvinced: 'It would've reacted with the nitrogen, the jug would've shattered.' These pitiless children's usual topic is how to dose Clod and Mum with enough drain-cleaner. They'll do it, too, one evening. It's just a question of choosing the right occasion, the right drink. Meanwhile they're cautious. Revenge on the older generation downstairs is only part of their idea. They want to be free, have no intention of seeing the inside of juvenile detention; their alibi's perfect, they're locked in their room; no one knows lithe little Rat long ago stole a key, that they come and go by night, that they horde ammonia in the filth beneath the chesterfield. '"Death by misadventure"', pronounces Bat luxuriously, their favourite phrase; just as their favourite game is playing at coroner's courts, Brat's teddybear standing in for Clod, Bunny playing Mum. Again and again they've examined those prone corpses, assessed the evidence of seared gut and blue face, and decided for 'A tragic muddling of bottles.' 'But what about Rat's fingerprints on the glasses?' mutters Bat, re-starting an old debate. 'We have to arson the house afterward.' She's Ginger's daughter, probably; the FitzRanulph strain is weakest in her, she has an instinct for criminal extremes. The other feel an attachment to their ancestral furniture. Nonetheless, the image of the house in flames, the four self-made orphans dancing about outside until the fire-engine comes and it's time to weep, is so gorgeous that they titter, stretching out small hands, knitting fingers in the darkness.

O doomed semi at Ware!

No surprises so far.

Angelo, in his grand hotel, has found a woman, or been found by one. Ms Jan Burgess is a Canadian of a certain age who was seated only a few barstools along from Serena. Jan was invisible to Serena, but Serena was all too visible to Jan, who watched through puckered eyes as she ignored Angelo, paid her bill, and sailed off into the night, cool and alone. Fortunately, Jan is used to the leavings of other women, and sun-tethered Angelo is used to falling in love punctually at nine, local time, when his shift behind the bar ends. Jan has already swept him upstairs to her room and bed, where she is doing everything *Cosmopolitan* and *Good Housekeeping* tell her she must do. As long as it lasts it's a polished performance, but her one desire is to get it over and done with, so she can enjoy pillow-talk on her one topic, reincarnation.

Reincarnation! It's not easy being a true believer. Women discuss previous lives in a competitive spirit – 'Oh, you remember the court of Cleopatra too? Perhaps you were one of my slaves' – while men are bored and won't listen at all unless bedded and, as it were, trapped. Such is Jan's experience. So what choice does she have? She *must* tell someone the story of her past existences. Story-telling is the only purpose of Jan's annual alimony-funded forays into Europe; her figure is arduously preserved by treadmill and bulimia for this sole end; for no other reason does she con the harlot magazines.

Angelo is a student of them also, like all good bartenders. If he concentrated, he could cite the *locus classicus* of each noise Jan makes, each gesture. That sudden thing with her knees is from last summer's bumper edition of the *Ladies' Home Journal*; moaning in his ear 'You gorgeous savage, never before ....' was recommended by *Fourteen!* in June 2013. But his mind, too, is not on the job. I'm sorry to say he's not thinking about Joanne at all. (*'Chi è?* Jeanne? Jane?'). He's thinking of that ruddy-haired Englishwoman who paid him no attention. '*Come una gran signora!'*

Jan, despite having been St Joan and Mary Queen of Scots, has never been thought enthralling. She has not enthralled once in the scores of times she has done what she is doing now. Nor will she enthrall any man as she repeats and repeats the deed (never forgetting to whisper 'You gorgeous savage *etcetera*') until she leaves this life and comes back – she zealously hopes – as someone better than a Winnipeg Buddhist. Perhaps a stint as a Brazilian supermodel? But won't the Brazilian supermodel be haunted by flashbacks of life as a dandruffy Canadian *divorcée*? Won't the Brazilian supermodel have to sleep with men to earn a fifteen minute audience for her memories of Winnipeg in the rain? What hope, then, of escaping from the cycle of more-or-less-shoddy lives into nirvana?

It's speculation of this sort that gives Jan her preoccupied air, and it's her preoccupied air that makes her easy to ignore, even in bed. Angelo groans politely, but these groans are uttered in his professional capacity as bartender. As a man he is absent, fixated on Serena. 'What intoxicating grace she had! Is she staying in this hotel?' (No.) 'Will I see her again?' (Never.) 'Why does she trouble me?'

Why does anyone trouble anyone? Why does anything happen? Characters fulfil their nature, and Nature fulfils herself through their vanity. Behaviour goes by rote. Even violent change only hurries us through the same cycle: *revolution* is the archest word in the language. Our guts are hammered to a point which we are forced to rotate, repeating and repeating until we are used up and the sacrifice is complete. Jan is an extreme case; Angelo is tethered to the same vortex, as are Tristan and Seb, although it does not hurt them much, or not yet. And Serena?

Serena has escaped, and not just Angelo. There are gratuitous exceptions to the vanity of our existence. Overhead the lunar escapade continues, after four-and-half-billion years or fifty-six billion months, and people, too, can play truant from original sin. By prank Serena has gone out of the hotel and down to the Arno. Now, at nine twenty-six, she is on the Ponte Santa Trìnita, swinging her handsome legs over the water, and watching the full moon stand still in those swift rippling waters. Despite everything she has been planning, she is remembering, a little mawkishly, her honeymoon in Crete. 'Ralphie,' she murmurs; against all expectation she finds herself pining for her dried-out, cringing husband. When he arrives in Florence tomorrow night he'll find her more vulnerable than he hoped, less astonished by his new manner than he might expect. They will be fairly happy together.

Nirav too has been delivered. His previous life is perfectly dead. The courageous new one is about to be formed (although already as lies in his snowy grave he hears, as from a million miles away, scraping above his frozen head). Meanwhile, at eight twenty-six, his being moves in places of which no light fiction speaks, far from his latent body, far also from the puny contents of his individual mind. In some uncatalogued manner he communes with his great-grandparents, the ones slain by their Muslim neighbours, with Kali the destroyer, on whom they called as they burned, and with the infinitesimal slumbering spirits of dormice.

Spurdle and Rawleigh have not escaped because they were never exactly bound. They continue in eccentric circles which, in their innocence, they do not understand as eccentric. At this moment ruddy Sir William Rawleigh, Bart., is drinking beer and discussing fodder with his grazier in the *Rawleigh Arms*. He has played the jovial squire for so many years the role now plays him; it must be said it plays him well, as well as it played his father and grandfather before him.

And at this moment the monks of Pluscarden Abbey, who have just finished chanting Compline and pulled their cowls over their heads, are going to bed. They process peacefully through their cloister, none more peacefully than Cuthbert, *né* Cedric Spurdle. Cedric is content to chant and walk predictably, to be a gap in the world, a gap for praise to be poured through. Above the shambling line of monks, moonlight falls through high unglazed windows, making silent splashes on the stones, and the splashes are exactly the huge shape they were a century ago, and five centuries before that.

At this moment, twenty-six minutes past eight, Ralph is by prank on his knees, digging with his long forgiving hands in the snow. The cold hurts him; his eyes prickle and swim in the black night, so he must work by feel. Yet he experiences a joy he hasn't come across before. he seems to be excavating a curious light, a thinning of darkness. It seems to him that he's digging down to paradise.

The captious moon gloats down on them all – there has never been such a moon – and even manages to ricochet off the Thames and penetrate beneath the prim curtains of an office high in the Palace of Westminster, casting a blue sheen on the already-not-unblue face of the Lord High Chancellor.

It would please me to display him to you meditating on the nature of law. But not a bit of it. He is peering peevishly at a list in his right hand, while his left hand fiddles with a mug of cocoa; and on the mug is painted a teddy-bear. The eyes of this teddy-bear catch the moon and gleam malevolently, which the Lord Chancellor does not perceive; nor does the sepulchral mandarin perching on a chair beside him, giving ear. O what a malevolent teddy it is. It isn't decently naked, but tricked out like a Victorian convict in white jacket, trousers and pillbox-hat, all peppered with broad black arrows. Below this bear we read, in scarlet gothic lettering, SPANK ME HARD.

LONDON REVIEW OF BOOKS: Is nothing sacred, m'Lud? Is nothing too cheap?

THE READER: Sustained.... Well I don't know. I admit a certain weariness myself. But I see there's only a page left. I am minded to let him conduct it in any way he sees fit.

AUTHOR: M'Lud.

'Gaunt-Blyghte' (sighs the Lord Chancellor, reading the list), 'oh yes I suppose so, Moxgrave dear me no, remove his name at once. Haggard, well all right. Shovell, Shovell, do I know Shovell? Oh *her*? Really? If you say so, but I *did* hope we could do better than that. What a shaming business, appointing red judges of Shovell's calibre. Gore? *Frances* Gore? I draw the line there, out she goes – no, Moulder, please don't look like that, I shan't be browbeaten. My cocoa's growing a skin and I need to go to bed.' Big Ben is telling the half hour, and the Lord Chancellor's Scotch nurse, long dead, still tyrannises his soul. Early hours, early hours! 'I'm taking a *firm line*. Bolswood. Bolswood, Sir Ralph Bolswood, no I don't recognise that name at all.'

'A newish silk, Lord Chancellor. Not very visible. Scarcely alive outside court, I should think.' Here the teddy winks moonlight. 'Contract law's his thing.'

'*Contract*? How very dull.'

'Yes, Lord Chancellor, but he's one of those sarcastic-cringing-vicious commercial lawyers. You know what happens to *them* once they're on the Bench. They sink their fangs into criminal cases and turn into draconian monsters.'

'That's all very well ....'

'And every single judge of the Queen's Bench Division detests him.'

'Do they just? *Do they?* Troublesome beasts. In that case I'll let him through. (Now, where do I sign?) I can't imagine one more obscure judge will do much harm,' but in fact Mr Justice Bolswood was soon proving a grievous disappointment on the Bench, not a mediocrity at all, voted deplorable throughout Whitehall, a standing irritation to the law-and-order Home Secretary, notorious even in the tabloids for his habit of mercy.

DR FELIX CULPEPPER WILL RETURN IN

PIRACIES